The Last Gambit

DAVID DELMAN

The Last Gambit

ST. MARTIN'S PRESS
NEW YORK

Library of Congress Cataloging-in-Publication Data

Delman, David.
    The last gambit : a case for Jacob Horowitz / David Delman.
       p.   cm.
    ISBN 0-312-05459-9
    I. Title.
  PS3554.E444L37   1991
  813'.54—dc20   90-15552
                                                 CIP

First published in Great Britain by William Collins Sons & Co. Limited

First U.S. Edition: March 1991
10 9 8 7 6 5 4 3 2 1

Annually, Cuba hosts the Capablanca Memorial Tournament, honouring José Raul Capablanca, one of the seminal figures in the development of modern chess. Though the Capa Open, held annually in Philadelphia, honours that same great master, it is entirely fictitious.

In memory of my father, who taught me the game. And for my grandchildren, to whom I taught it.

Part One

OPENINGS

In chess when a player has to move, but cannot do so without damage to his position, he is said to be in *zugzwang*. And *zugzwang* doth make cowards of us all.

S.S. (Foxy) Farrington

CHAPTER 1

Lanie found him in the hotel coffee shop, at breakfast. It was late, almost ten, and the large room had that slightly hollow sound that comes from being sparsely filled. On the table a copy of the *Philadelphia Sentinel* was open to 'Farrington on Chess', and Dimmie was bent over it—it, and the hot, rich cereal that was one of his passions. He ate quickly, as he did most things. Quick, yet never awkward—that was her Dimmie. Except, of course, he wasn't really hers any longer, if, in fact, he ever had been. She sat down next to him.

He glanced at her, then away, not glad to see her, but too innately polite to let that show. Briefly she caressed his cheek.

'You slept well last night?' he asked.

She thought of lying—for the sake of being pleasant together—but it got away from her. 'No,' she said. 'The room was empty without you. The bed was, too. I've been thinking, Dimmie—why don't I see about a suite? You could move in, and it would be big enough so I wouldn't be under foot all the time.'

He compressed his lips.

Hers widened in a desperately chipper smile. 'Never mind,' she said hurriedly. 'It was just a thought, but if it's not a good idea, why then we'll stay as we are.'

'Lanie, I asked you not to come, and you said you wouldn't. You said you understood that total concentration was necessary and no distractions. You said you understood all that, and yet you're here.'

'Yes.'

'Why are you?'

'I couldn't help myself.'

He pushed the cereal aside unfinished and reached for his coffee cup.

'Shall I have it freshened?' she asked, looking around for a waitress.

'It's fine.'

'It's probably tepid by now, and you hate—'

'It's fine, it's fine. It's just the way I like it. The best chefs in Europe, giving it their all, couldn't make it one whit better. Lanie, go home.'

'But I came to play in the tournament.'

'You didn't. You came to make it difficult for me to play in it.'

She said nothing, eyes fixed on the tabletop, hoping he wouldn't see they were beginning to fill. After a moment or so he took her hand. 'Please, please don't do that.'

'Isn't *she* a distraction?'

'Who?'

'Have you seen her? Don't lie to me, Dimmie. You don't have to, you know.'

He drew his hand away. 'No,' he said. 'I haven't seen her.'

'Have you tried to?'

'Yes, damn it, I've tried to. But she won't take calls from me. She's smarter than you. She knows what a low-life I am.'

'I read her column this morning. It was about that little boy with AIDS, who they won't let in school. She writes so well. She writes as if she cares about things. She must be such a nice person.'

He didn't answer.

'Dimmie . . .?'

'What?'

'I know you love her. I've seen you try to hide that, even from yourself, but it's so just the same. Still, that doesn't absolutely mean she's the best person in the world for you, does it? Suppose she doesn't really and truly love you?'

'I've told you again and again, that's all over. Done with. It's merely that I have some of her letters. If she knew I still had them she'd want them back.'

'Can't you just—'

'No,' he said. He'd been toying with a plastic spoon, and now, savagely, he broke it in half. 'If she wants them the least she can do is—' He stopped, inhibited by what he himself recognized as spurious. 'Lanie, Lanie, leave it alone, for God's sake. Who are you, the KGB?'

She made a frantic grab for the chess problem. 'Mate in two,' she said. 'Did you solve it, Dimmie? Of course you did.'

He let his breath out heavily. 'I've made you cry again.'

'No, you haven't. I swear you haven't.'

'Twice in five minutes. That's a record even for the great Dmitri Kaganovich. Lanie, sweetheart, don't let me do this to you any more. Unload me. Pack me in. Find someone who—'

'There isn't anyone,' she said. 'And there never will be.'

'Christ,' he said and banged the table hard enough to startle two middle-aged ladies in print dresses who then turned towards him, hungry for the drama he seemed to promise.

Clicking his heels, he bowed to them and left.

As he often did when troubled, he headed for his beautiful car, found it in the parking lot, patted it, said something loving to it, and got in. A short time later he was on the turnpike going north. His foot on the accelerator became heavier, troubles lighter—80 . . . 85 . . . God, how he adored speed. You could play it with . . . *state cops*. He slackened pressure, amused as always at his instinct to be good. Some swashbuckler, he said of himself derisively.

Settling in at a civilized 65, he thought of his father, long dead now, whose assessment of his only son had been bleak. Not for Ilya a perspective that would permit 'good' in the picture. 'The hangman's rope is what you'll end on'— a prophecy put forward in broken English during the Brook-

lyn years and, with increasing frequency, in fluent, emphatic
Russian after the exodus. It was their last confrontation
Dimmie conjured up. With the clarity of yesterday (not
eighteen years ago) he could see the dank, dingy kitchen of
the minuscule apartment on Dnieper Street—Momma and
Manya, his younger sister, banished so the bull Kagano-
viches could lock horns as was their wont. Seventeen-year-
old Dimmie seated at the table, awaiting the reckoning; the
patriarch at the window, staring out at abstractions, hands
clasped behind his back, still silent—but both knew the
nature of the storm that was gathering.

At last he turned, hulking and ominous. 'So . . . are you
going to marry her? Smetsov says you made him a promise.
Did you?'

'Yes.'

'Why?'

'He had a hammer in his hand.'

Six inches taller than his son, thirty pounds heavier, a
cossack of a man, Ilya reached the far end of the room in a
bound. Swung open a cabinet, tore a calendar off the door,
hurled it to the table like a thunderbolt: 'Look!'

Dimmie looked, saw three tiny red marks over days
spaced a week apart and knew instantly what they signified.

'Tell me what you see,' Ilya demanded.

'Three tiny red marks.'

It was not of course the answer Ilya wanted, but it *was*
the answer calculated to inflame him. Dimmie delivered it as
if programmed. Press the impudence button and impudence
comes out. He waited, joylessly, for it to have its impact.
He didn't have to wait long. The calendar was slammed
viciously over his head.

'Three times!' Ilya roared, calendar connecting serially.
'Three separate times I warned you she was a scheming
trollop. Is that not true?'

Dimmie nodded.

'Speak, you idiot!'

'Yes, you warned me.'

'Three times I sat you down here and said to you, the neighbourhood is on fire with what a fool Ilya Kaganovich's son is about to make of himself with the tramp Olga Smetsov. How many times?'

'Three.'

The rolled-up calendar counted them off on Dimmie's head, eliciting soft female sounds of protest—a kind of keening—from another part of the apartment. Ilya paid no heed. Breathing hard, he sat down opposite Dimmie, staring at him. But suddenly he seemed exhausted, face pale, hands visibly trembling.

'I don't understand you,' he said, voice heavy with despair. 'I never have, and I suppose I never will.'

Dimmie agreed that that was so but wordlessly.

'It can't be you *want* the little Smetsov for a wife. No one could. Crooks, connivers, nothings, the Smetsovs. And yet you, the son of Engineer Kaganovich, willingly, *eagerly*, place yourself in a position where they can make you responsible. You *know* the girl is with child?'

'Yes.'

'*Is* it yours?'

'It might be.' He paused. 'Or it might be Stefan's.'

Ilya watched him.

'Or Fyodor's.' And then he named four other potential sires.

'Oh God, it's a *game*,' Ilya said, groaning. But it was not to his son he spoke. It was to himself, or to some other Great Auditor, as if in explanation. 'I should have known. It's one of his infernal, everlasting games.' Now he looked at Dimmie. 'There is money involved?'

Dimmie nodded. 'A lot. The winner will be able to go to Moscow, to study with Valentin Gregorin. And there is no better chess teacher in the world.'

'And the loser?'

Dimmie shrugged. 'Won't be me.'

Ilya's silence was profound, full of the unspoken—this time—exasperation and hopelessness that sooner or later he was always reduced to by his son's astonishing effervescence.

But Dimmie was proof against mere silence, no matter how profound. Gripped by irrepressible excitement, he said, 'Tomorrow's the drawing. Long straw goes to Moscow, short one to the altar.' His grin blazed up. 'If you're through with me, Poppa, I'm on my way to the muni-building to find out about train schedules.'

The next day he drew the long straw as he had known he would, but the good news never reached Ilya. Dimmie arrived home with it too late. Ilya had been found slumped over his desk at the engineering works an hour before, dead of a heart attack.

A Mercedes toyed with him tauntingly for about five miles, a frisky BMW gave him a horn toot while its young driver forwarded a look of challenge, but Dimmie resisted both, saying, inwardly, 'I pick my own games to play.' Sedately, then, he guided his marvellous car from middle to fast lane and back again as the occasion warranted.

What an odd son for Ilya Kaganovich to have had, Dimmie thought. Ilya, so straight and convention-bound. 'Life is *not* a game,' he had said so often, roaring the words as if God Himself were a waverer. Accompanying the stricture from time to time with therapy from his belt or his meaty hand.

Wrong, so wrong, Dimmie thought. That's exactly what life was—a crazy, complex game that a few learned to play with some skill and that everyone eventually lost. But you could end it whenever you pleased, discard it like unlucky dice if and when you wearied of it.

Trenton. (He'd go one more exit before turning back.) And now he thought of Buddy—and saying things like that to her, honest things, daring things, things it had never occurred to him to say before, certainly not to any other woman. For instance: that sex was the *optimum* game, the best chase, the highest competitive excitement. And then, waiting, with some trepidation, to see the extent of the penalty he'd have to pay for stripping away the mask.

'You really are a clod, Dmitri.'

'Why? Because I name names? I'm a clod because I know the thrill of the fuck for what it is. Because I refuse to romanticize it into a greeting card?'

She burrowed into him and kissed the warm place at the base of his throat, making shivery music up and down his spine. 'No, my Russian Don Juan, that's not why you're a clod.'

'Then why?'

'Clods are clods because they vulgarly miss the point.'

'I see.'

She got up on an elbow and studied him. 'The point is *I* wanted you.'

He returned the car to the parking lot, said au revoir to it, and walked towards the hotel entrance. A pair of teen-agers in Capa Open T-shirts were basking in the sun and playing chess. One of them recognized him, called to him, and he joined them at their bench. They were both pretty good. For the next ten minutes he enjoyed their battle and when it was over, said, 'Half a buck a game. I play minus my queen, and the two of you play as a team. Done?' They agreed. He stayed two hours and won three dollars.

CHAPTER 2

Barney Hogan poured a beer and a shot for Hank the Postman, and came back up the bar to Buddy. He looked at her hard, the way he always did when he suspected all was not right with her world and that she was being secretive about the details.

'I'll take what Hank did,' she said.

'The hell you will.'

'Just kidding.'

'What are you doing here this time of morning anyway?'

'What time of morning is it?'

He showed her his watch, which indicated that the sun had at least a couple of hours before it could be construed as over the yardarm.

'OK, then I'll have a cup of coffee,' she said. 'Aren't you glad to see me?'

He grumbled something affirmative as he went to get the coffee but made it clear he thought he was being flirted with. He hated that, and she knew he did because he had told her so, often. 'You use it as a device,' he told her. 'You never flirt except when you want to hide something. Friends don't need devices. Any time you want me to back off or butt out, say so, and I'll do it,' he insisted. And she believed he believed every word.

'It's the damn column,' she said. 'I've rewritten it twice now, glibness and banality rolling trippingly off the word processor. The best thing that could happen to me is writer's block.'

Knowing her pattern—anxiety seldom very far from her door—he said, 'You're probably—what, three, four columns ahead?'

'And now you're going to suggest something sensible as hell—like why don't I grab a cab down to the pier and do some boat-watching.'

'Yeah, that's what I was going to suggest.'

'Or better still I could take a personal day and watch the boats from my apartment window, the occasional gin and tonic handy for added therapy.'

'Better still,' he said.

'You're such a clever old Barney.' With a gentle tweak of his nose.

He slapped her hand away and left her for a moment to pour himself a cup of coffee. When he returned he said, 'There was a guy in here last night—Kaganovich, he said his name was, looking for you.'

'*Pour moi?*'

'He's in town for the Capa Open, he says. What's that, one of the real biggie tournaments in the world of chess?'

'Could be. I don't really know a lot about the world of chess. God, this coffee's strong.'

'Is it?'

'You run such a male domain, Barney. Even your damn coffee is for men only.'

He swabbed at the counter. 'Nice enough sort of guy, Kaganovich. Dimmie. That's what everybody calls him, he said. He was here almost three hours, till closing time. Place wasn't crowded. Told me his life story.'

'How lovely for you.'

'Pretty colourful stuff. Says he knows you pretty well. Says you told him a lot about me, but he knew a lot anyway, he says, because he's a baseball nut. Says he was there the night I got my last strikeout, against the Giants. Says it was a slider down and Mays missed it a foot.' He smiled. 'Hard not to like a guy who remembers that good.'

She covered her mouth to obscure a yawn. 'Guess I better be getting back to the office,' she said. 'I've got a column to write, you know.'

'How come you never told me about this Dimmie?'

She shrugged.

He waited.

She glared at him. 'Some of Buddy Horowitz's life belongs to Buddy Horowitz and no one else. *No* one else, not even you, Barney. I don't mean it to come as a shock to you, but I'm a P.R.I.V.A.T.E. person.'

'Sure as spitballs,' he said.

'Then why ask?'

They were both silent for a moment but then she reached for him and pulled him towards her to kiss where she had previously tweaked. 'I'll give you chapter and verse sometime,' she said. 'Not just yet, OK?'

She finished her coffee. 'Ugh,' she said. 'Doctor Barney dollink, in your inimitable way you've done me good, despite this warlock's brew.'

'He's got some of your letters, Buddy.'

She stared at him for a moment. 'Oh God,' she said. 'He

kept them. He swore he wouldn't. We promised each other
to burn—Oh hell, I might have known he'd lie to me about
that, too.'

'Do you want them back, the letters, I mean.'

'No.'

'You're sure?'

'I just want them never to have existed.' She shivered.
'The thing about those letters is they make me feel ashamed.'

CHAPTER 3

When Fielding Gow unlatched his door and discovered it
was Deirdre who had knocked he should have been surprised
but wasn't. She'd surprised him last when she was eight by
informing him that he was her one true love and that he'd
best plan on forsaking all others. He'd been twelve at the
time. It had been during a Little League baseball game.
She'd marched purposefully from grandstand to boy-packed
bench to deliver her message—negligible body pencil
straight, mouth set and determined as a drill sergeant's.
Nor had she whispered, or made any other attempt to be
decently discreet. A posting of the banns is what it had
been, as if in response to a sudden need to unclutter the
record. In the aftermath he remembered: (1) giggling and
guffawing team mates, (2) his own fierce, hot blush, and (3)
that she hadn't once looked back though he repeatedly
yelled 'Redheaded greaseball' at her for all the world to
hear.

Through the years, however, he had learned to accept
her for what she was, a person defined by her own unpredict-
ability. Actually, he'd become so entranced by that aspect
of her it made all other women seem bland by comparison.
Still, she *was* supposed to be in London. In exile there, to
put the matter in its operative context.

'Understand me,' her father had said. 'I could squash

this now, which is what I really want to do. I won't hide
that from either of you. I make no bones about the fact that
in my view Fielding is a loser.'

This view was not of course new to Fielding, and he tried
hard to keep his face expressionless when the cold grey eyes
bored into his. He believed he was reasonably successful,
despite the customary internal shrinking.

'I don't want to hear that any more, Daddy,' Deirdre had
said. 'Fielding is nothing of the kind. And as for squashing—
to use *your* ugly term—the only power you have over us is
what *he* gives you. Because if it were up to me we would
have eloped long ago. Besides, we both know that's not
what this is really about, don't we?'

He kept silent.

'Daddy . . .?'

'Six months,' he said as if she hadn't spoken. 'No contact
between you of any kind. When Deirdre returns from London, perhaps we'll discuss this again.'

'I don't think so,' Fielding had said and left them.

Deirdre caught up to him just as he reached the lion
couchant at the top of their outside steps. He'd been almost
running, she almost flying.

'You wait up, Fielding Gow.'

He did. That is, his body did. She knew him well enough
to perceive distinctions.

'I could hate you,' she said. 'You make it so easy for him.'

'Why not? He's right. I am a loser.'

'He doesn't care about that. That's smokescreen, and you
know it. What he cares about is you're a Gow.'

'Maybe it's the same thing,' he said and stepped away
from her.

But she grabbed his arm. 'Damn you, you don't believe
that. What your father did he paid for. He suffered. It might
even be what killed him. He . . . Oh hell, Fielding, the point
is that what he did *he* did. It wasn't you. It had nothing to
do with you, and my father can't make it your cross to bear
unless you let him.'

He looked at her, then shook his head. 'Don't you ever have doubts? You're absolutely amazing. There are no greys in your world. Only blacks and whites. Everything is so damned easy.'

'I know what I want, if that's what you mean. But all right, I've decided to be good. I'm being beautifully, marvellously good. I'm giving him his six months. I'm giving them to you, too. And then that's it. No more, I'm warning both of you.'

'Goodbye, Deirdre.'

'Don't you *dare* use that word to me.'

He moved past her.

'And don't you do anything stupid while I'm gone,' she shouted after him. 'I mean, Fielding, you damn well better be waiting where I can find you.'

He started down the stairs.

'Fielding . . .'

'What?'

'Say you love me.'

'No.'

'*Say* it.'

'I don't love you. Or me. Or anything.'

And he'd gone.

Of the six months she'd agreed to only a month and a half had passed, and yet here she was at his door. That was his first thought. His next—despite himself—concerned his own general seediness, exemplified by the stained T-shirt, and the three-day growth of beard. She, on the other hand, looked so emphatically clean. Even as an adolescent— in her time of knobby-kneed lankness and unredeemed flatness—she had always had this way of glistening. Nothing flat about her now. And lankness had become long-legged litheness, but that was not news to him either.

'Hello, Fielding,' she said, steaming forward as if to slip the blockade. He did not, however, move out of the way, and she was forced to drop anchor.

'What happened to London?' he asked.

She placed her palm on his chest and shoved with enough force to tip his balance, then slithered past him.

'Princess Royal,' he said to her bitterly. 'Always were, always will be. Have to have your own way. Can't take no for an answer. Concentrate, your highness. I—don't—want—you—HERE!'

She ignored him proficiently. He was not surprised at that either, she was a chronic sufferer from selective deafness.

Having achieved the centre of the room, she stood there surveying its pervasive nastiness: junkyard furniture, peeling wallpaper, cracked window-panes, clutter of newspapers and magazines, unmade bed, and, inevitably, dirty dishes in the kitchen sink.

She said nothing, but the extent of her disdain was instantly communicated, and that instantly infuriated him. He grabbed her arm, intending forcible ejection. She wriggled free.

'Don't you put your filthy paws on me,' she said.

'Then take off.'

'Look at this place, it's a sty. No wonder nobody knows where you are. You're too ashamed.'

'The hell I'm ashamed. I live the way I want to live, and it's nobody's goddam business but mine.'

'I called everyone I could think of. I called your friends the Parrishes. I even called my father, for heaven's sake. Everyone said you'd disappeared.'

He went to the door and flung it open so vigorously that it bounced back and had to be re-opened. 'I want *you* to disappear. Out! Now! I don't want to have to hurt you, but I will if that's what it takes.'

'Pig,' she said.

He moved towards her again, more carefully this time.

'Oink-oink,' she said.

Inch by inch he manœuvred her towards the far wall, near the bathroom door. He had his eye on that, aware that it was an avenue of retreat. His plan was to herd her away so that she couldn't make a dash for it and lock herself in.

Suddenly she head-faked in that direction. Suckered, he was thrust off balance when she slammed into him, knees driving. body pressing, arms tight around his neck, mouth glued on his. And he couldn't shake her loose. He felt the sweet pliancy of her hips, the indescribable softness of her breasts, and the powerful—lickety-split—surge of his own response. She felt that, too, and ended the kiss to grin triumphantly. After which she began shucking off her clothes.

'You're crazy,' he said.

Unzipping him, she reached for what was there and led him by it to the bed.

'Deirdre, no. It's ended. Let it goddam stay that way this time.'

'I didn't end anything. All I agreed to was a recess.'

'This is a mistake.'

Inexorably, she drew him on.

'Your father will kill me. And I wouldn't blame him.'

'My father is only my father,' she said. 'I'll worry about my father.'

'For Christ's sake, at least let me shower.'

But even for that she would not free him.

CHAPTER 4

'I, Dimitri Kaganovich, son of Svetlana and Ilya Kaganovich, while of sound mind and . . .'

He stopped, read what he had written, then underscored *sound mind*. He thought about that for a moment, crossed the words out entirely, and crumpled the paper into a ball. He flung this towards the trash basket, which was already piled so high it looked like a pop art ice-cream cone. The ball banked of the surface and rolled across the rug to join a quartet of forerunners. He started over.

'I, Dimitri Leonid Kaganovich, contemplating the taking of my life, absolve . . .'

He stopped again. 'Shit,' he said aloud. The quintet became a sextet.

He got up from the desk and went to the window. City Avenue, ugly with afternoon traffic, prodded a memory he couldn't quite track at first, and then he did. The scene was, uncannily, the model for one of those anti-US posters that used to festoon the classrooms of the Petroska School bearing captions like: 'How America lives.' Or: 'Behold the joys of capitalism.'

'A plutocrat is a technocrat with decadence in his guts,' Professor Bolganov—grey teeth, pipestem legs—loved to say, hopping cricket-like between poster and blackboard where he had scrawled those words, pointing the moral with the flat of his revered Red Army bayonet.

Only sixteen-year-old Dimmie, transplanted Yank, had chosen to take issue, arguing that to have a traffic problem one must first have cars. As a result he, too, achieved a special relationship with the flat of the Red Army bayonet.

Young Dimmie, full of beans and optimism then, to whom suicide was a word he could spell, but absurd to think it might ever pertain beyond that.

Well, did it? Was he in any way serious about it, or was it just another example of 'Dimmie's dementia', to use Valentin Gregorin's phrase?

'Like all compulsive gamesters, you're a coward, Dimmie,' Gregorin had said on a night when they were drunk and loquacious together.

Dimmie, sprawled in a chair next to him, had lifted the pistol from his lap, attempting with liquor-numbed lips to form the words: Russian Roulette.

Though he was only partially successful, Gregorin had understood. 'No, no, in that way you're brave enough. *Existentially*, you're a sniveller, if you know what I mean.'

Dimmie had not.

'Rules restrain chaos,' Gregorin had said. 'Games are built on rules. Thus, consciously or not, gamesters are gamesters out of a desperate need for an ordered universe.

You, my friend, are mad for games because you cannot tolerate the idea of nothingness. The Void makes your knees knock and explains as well Dimmie's dementia.'

'Dimmie's what?'

'Pass the cognac, tovarich.'

In the morning he had asked Gregorin to recap the previous night's discourse, but by then the latter needed prodding to recall even vaguely the outlines of what he had said and professed to have no idea as to what he might have meant.

But if suicide was a game, what kind of game could it be? How could you win? Did winning have something to do with making one's death extraordinary in some way? 'A death of importance,' he said aloud, enjoying the sonorous sound of it.

Returning to the desk, he got his chess computer out of the drawer and fooled around with it a bit. Getting better all the time, these electronic savants; not good enough yet to beat the loftiest grand masters, but good enough to worry shit out of us, Dimmie acknowledged. Two years of grace, their programmers were warning. Dimmie lifted the black queen, miniaturized but sweetly shaped. He stared at her balefully. Unnatural bitch, can't leave us to our hard-won expertise, can you? Determined to bring us down, right? Make eunuchs of us all, as it were. *En garde*—and with a flourish switched off her battery. He began replaying Bernstein versus Mieses, 1904, which he had always liked, regarding it as a vivid example of how to control much with little.

The phone rang. Boris Tsarkov's heavy voice said, 'I wish to speak to the crumbum Dmitri Kaganovich.'

'Sorry. You'll have to repeat that.'

'You don't understand English, you crumbum?'

'Pigs like you can't talk English. They can only talk pig-talk.'

The mouthpiece at the other end was covered, and when it was clear again he heard the elegant English of V.

Gregorin. He was informed by him that the tourney's Skittles Room had opened early and that Tsarkov had expressed an interest in taking money from Kaganovich. Was Kaganovich averse to blitz chess at five dollars a game?

'When?'

'An hour.'

'I'll be there.'

'Dimmie . . .'

'Yes?'

In Russian: 'What makes you torture him so?'

In English: 'Pig-sticking turns me on.'

He allowed Bernstein to finish Mieses, thinking that games with only pawns left really were easier to win. Even Tsarkov paid lip-service to that, but Kaganovich didn't believe he believed it. Tsarkov, brilliant though he was, had no heart for the kind of drawn-out end game that could drain a man hollow, at least not with Dimmie across the board from him. Or so it had been once. It would be interesting to see if things had changed. For a moment he felt a blood surge—in the old way—at the smell of competition. But it lasted only long enough to irritate. Not for the first time, then, he decided it had been a mistake to come to this of all cities and enter the Open. A hot flash. An act of mid-life crisis somewhat before the fact.

Dispiritedly, he lay down on the bed. He placed his hands behind his head and stared at the phone, willing it to ring, willing it to be Buddy. He worked out various scenarios, little miracles of sweetness and light. There was one he liked particularly. In it he made her understand how unequivocally he still loved her, never mind that his behaviour had been . . . well, equivocal at best. Something in his voice, not the words, but the timbre, the *music* of his voice, was so persuasive that . . .

He swung himself erect, pushed the phone buttons.

'Buddy Horowitz here.'

Distinctive; slightly throaty; Cleopatra might have had a voice like that, he thought.

'Buddy,' he said. 'Listen to me. I—'

She hung up.

He lay back on the bed. After a while he got up and crossed the room to the desk again.

'I, Dmitri L. Kaganovich, in his . . .'

Part Two

MID-GAME

The effect of an isolated pawn is to spread gloom over the chessboard.

Savielly Tartakower

CHAPTER 1

Only weeks separated Jacob Horowitz's last two conversations with his cousin Buddy, but as he put down the phone he decided the interval felt much longer. It felt, actually, as if some kind of fission had taken place, resulting in a pair of Buddies barely on nodding terms with each other. Where were warmth and friendliness? Properties endemic to Buddy One, they seemed non-existent in Buddy of the second part.

'I swear there's nothing prettier than a three-four-three double-play,' Helen called to him from the lounge chair in the den.

Herself a former mainstay of Southwestern University's female Rangers, Helen Horowitz was a serious watcher of the New York Mets. Just then, however, she had seen no double-play involving a grounder to first, a toss to second, and a return flip to first. In fact she had seen no double-play at all. What it was was smokescreen, generated to obscure the intensity with which she'd been eavesdropping.

He came into the den to sit on the arm of her chair. 'She'll be glad to have me stay,' he said.

'Oh?'

'She did sound a bit strained,' he acknowledged.

'A bit?' Outrage blew away smokescreen: 'I got the impression she thought you were Jake the Leper.'

He stroked her hair. 'I wish you liked her more.'

Irritated shrug.

'The thing is you ought to like her.'

'Why? Because we're both former jocks? I hated Annie Devlin, who was our team captain for three years. She was a big, well-coordinated cow. I hated her with a passion.'

'What I had in mind,' he said patiently, 'is that you usually do like people who are smart, honest, loyal . . .'

She hopped on loyal. 'To her best friend, who happens to be your former wife, the effect of which is she's yet to call me by my first name. Actually, to her I don't have a name. I have a designation: Other Woman.'

'Helen—'

'All right, I'm exaggerating. It's not that bad, but it is bad.'

'Fact: She *has* called you by your first name.'

'She slurs it. Slurring doesn't count.'

'Fact: Shirley and I were a lost cause before I ever set eyes on you.'

'You know that, I know that, and probably Buddy knows it, too. She just chooses not to let it get in her way.' Heaving herself into motion, she was headed for the kitchen on a mission of an obscure nature when suddenly she stopped and pivoted like the shortstop she once had been. Without breaking stride she shoved Jacob into the chair just vacated so that she could conveniently put her arms around his neck. 'I *know* she means a lot to you. She was after all the first female to worship at your shrine, and men never forget the women who think they're perfect.'

He muttered something mildly self-deprecating.

She kissed the top of his head where the hair was beginning to thin and decided not to tease him about that. 'The truth is I do like her, and I think she might like me, too, under ordinary circumstances. But you get in the way, my love. We're both possessive women, and we haven't figured out yet how much of you we're willing to share.'

Jacob scowled. He delighted in being a bone of contention but knew it was wiser to pretend he didn't.

'Now I better go up and pack,' she said with a valedictory kiss of the thin spot. Pause and a second thought: 'Jacob, maybe you better start combing your hair strategically.'

And so he knew she had caught him pretending.

He followed her. While she filled her suitcase they discussed logistics. Helen had a morning plane to catch. It would take her to Chicago where an old friend was about to become a client. In what way precisely she wasn't absolutely sure.

'I need a private detective, and you're the best I know' was all George Adams had said during their three-minute phone conversation. But he'd sounded worried. That surprised her because she'd always thought him among the most unflappable of men. Adams was an investment banker, CEO of a multi-national corporation with multi-complex security problems. Was it something along those lines? Probably. And yet she had never known him to be knocked off stride by anything concerning his business.

'Give me a hint,' she had said. 'I need something to tell Jacob.'

'Why?'

She thought of the array of answers she could give to that, all having to do with the nature of the attraction that existed between them—powerful on his side, and on her side undeniably present. She would not lie to herself about that. Nor would she to Jacob if he should ever put the direct question to her—he hadn't yet. Attraction, however, was one matter. What was done about it was another entirely, a conviction of hers that was bedrock when it came to the defining of things. But all she said to Adams was: 'You know why.'

'Yes. He thinks I have designs on you. He's right, of course, but they're on temporary hold.' The line went silent a moment, and then in one of his driest tones—Adams, a man who hated histrionics, owned a whole range of dry tones—he said, 'It seems Deirdre has been kidnapped.'

'Seems?'

'There's been a note.'

'So why seems?'

'I'll tell you when you get here.'

'Just tell me what the note said.'

'When you get here.' And hung up.

Jacob, too, would leave the Tri-Towns next morning (Thursday) but not on business. He would be driving the ninety miles to Philadelphia, city of his birth, to compete in a chess tournament. It would be his novice effort. Scheduled as a five-day event, the tournament, called the Capa Open, after Capablanca, one of chess's legendary figures, was designed in two sections: great players in the top bracket, modest ones in the bottom. For the great players it was an event of significance inasmuch as the winner would take home $20,000, very big money for a chess tournament. For the patzers (the uncharitable term popularized by Bobby Fischer) first prize was $1000, plus of course the thrill of victory.

After an extended hiatus Jacob had returned to chess three years ago. His father had taught him rules and moves when he was eight. An OK game, Jacob had thought, but in terms of emotive power simply not in it with baseball, for which he shared his wife's passion. To this reaction his father's reaction had been complex. Louis Horowitz had always regarded his own response to chess as bordering on the disastrous. There had been periods when it had interefered with his pursuit of a livelihood, when it had disrupted his marriage and other relationships, brief but painful periods when it had overwhelmed him like the addiction which in his case it plainly was. As a result, Louis was in part relieved to see Jacob immune. Yet disappointed, too. In one of his fantasies father and favourite son played chess harmlessly through the years, drawn ever closer by ritual and mystery, ties of blood strengthened by a mutual fascination. In a passive way Jacob had known this, though Louis never spoke of it. At the time of Louis's death three years ago, however, the knowledge had suddenly become poignant.

'Jacob, what?' Helen demanded.

'Nothing. Foolishness.'

'I saw your face. Tell me.'

'My father,' he said. 'You know.'

'And something else,' she said. And then guessed: 'Farrington!'

Hammer on the nail, he recognized at once. Subconsciously, true enough, but Helen no longer needed road maps to find her way around that murky country.

Simon (Foxy) Farrington was Jacob's *bête noire*, and no visit to Philadelphia since the re-entry of chess into his life had been free of confrontation. Farrington, a one-time prodigy, loved beating Jacob. The two shared an enmity singularly instinctual, patterned closely on the mutuality between mongeese and snakes. Both were members of the Quaker Chess Club. It was there that Farrington stalked Jacob with the kind of dedication that was little short of ferocious. Farrington's chess columns—appearing weekly in the *Philadelphia Sentinel*—were noteworthy for the waspishness with which they held error up to ridicule. His victories over Jacob were often grist for these. Yet something in Jacob, something visceral, kept him from any behaviour that might be described as evasive. But, as the world knew, Foxy never played in tournaments. Jacob kept reminding himself of this. It helped; it somehow failed to cure.

'Farrington,' Helen said, following this with an Apache spitting sound. 'What am I going to do with you, Jacob?'

'Maybe a hug?'

'Maybe an exorcist,' she said. 'If you come back from Philadelphia with that half-crazy little dybbuk still a factor in our lives I'm going to get serious, you hear me?'

He affirmed that he had.

For awhile then they discussed office politics as they existed in the homicide branch of the Tri-Towns police department. Jacob was an acknowledged star there. Acknowledged not merely in the Tri-Towns, but in the great metropolis only thirty miles away. New York City journalists liked Jacob. They liked his wit, his irreverence, and his iconoclastic approach to red tape. Consistently, he made good copy for them, and on four glittering occasions he had cracked cases important enough—or lurid enough—to have attracted national attention.

So star he was. And acknowledged he was, too, even by

those to whom star quality (in others) was a sign (in others) of unseemly ambition. Theodore H. Knudsen, a one-time police chief and now Tri-Towns' mayor was in the vanguard of that list. Suspicious as only a political animal could be, he watched Jacob gimlet-eyed, blocking what he could—and delaying what he couldn't block—of perquisites and promotion. But the mayor was wrong about Jacob, who was *not*, truly, a career-minded man. And though certainly Knudsen could irritate him from time to time, by and large the mayor's exorbitant anxiety about him amused Jacob. It did not amuse Helen. Nor did Jacob's amusement amuse her either. In her view Knudsen was that ever-hateful combination of bully and craven. It was a crying shame that Jacob let him get away with what he did, when with a little effort . . .

'Enough already,' Jacob said.

Helen sighed, realizing that was probably true—at least for now.

After a while she asked, 'Did Captain Cox do a number on you about time off?'

Jacob explained that he'd caught a break, that with the mayor on one of his periodic West Coast junkets, Cox was out from under temporarily. 'Without hizzoner, Cox is a different Cox,' he said.

Before striking out in a private way six months earlier, Helen too had been a working cop under Dennis Cox. She thoroughly liked and respected him, but it was a case of warts and all. 'Cox is Cox,' she said. 'And if you had asked for three days off instead of two, he would have reverted to type.'

She zipped up her duffle-bag and swung it off the bed. He watched her, admiring the easy strength and grace of all her movements. She was a big woman, wide in the shoulders and staunch through the hips and legs—a big, graceful woman in her forties, who on certain days—this one, for instance—seemed to him almost achingly beautiful. And seemed to him, after eight years of marriage, not much changed from the Sheriff H. Blye who had narrowed her eyes at him as he entered her neat-as-a-pin office for the first time. A cold, unwelcoming stare, he had always insisted. A careful scrutinizing glance was her descriptive term, adding that it could hardly have been otherwise, considering the circumstances. Small (southwestern) town sheriff meets hot-shot, big city cop. Put-downs and patronizing absolutely predictable, she told him. Had they materialized? No, she admitted. Of course not, because it was love at first sight (on his part) and she should have known it. Well, actually she had, she said, which was why she'd permitted . . . and so on. A nostalgic litany familiar and pleasant to them both.

Suddenly, out of nowhere, sadness struck Jacob, the sadness of separation in enervating waves. He felt, for some reason, ashamed of this and tried not to let it show. She saw it anyway.

'Jacob,' she said. 'Don't. It's only for a week.'

'Adams will keep you there longer if he can.'

'I won't let him. One week, I promise. A one-week assignment, I told him, no matter what. And he knows me well enough to take that seriously.'

'Yeah, he knows you, but not as well as he wants to know you.'

'Jacob, Jacob.'

'What's so funny?'

'You. So cool, everybody thinks. And here you are.'

'Here I am what?'

'Jealous.'

'Damn it, it's our first separation.'

This was untrue, but she chose not to correct the record. Instead she took him to bed where they honoured vigorously their first separation that wasn't.

CHAPTER 2

Barney Hogan's was one of those friendly bars often found near newspaper buildings because newspaper people like friendly bars. Or have a way of transmogrifying perfectly ordinary bars into friendly bars to suit their purposes. At any rate it was dark and clean—large enough to accommodate a ten-table dining annexe. It was called Dugout, since Barney was a former Philadelphia Phillies relief pitcher. Past sixty now, he was not easily relatable to the slim young stalwart who grinned down at patrons from a framed photograph mounted between crossed baseball bats, in which none other than Willie Mays had an arm about his shoulders. In a single glowing year that young stalwart had established Major League records for strikeouts *and* successive strikeouts in an All-Star game. After that his career had sputtered, then died, and in due time both his records had been eclipsed. 'K', however (the official scorer's symbol for strike-out) still lingered in his nickname, though few who used it could recall the glory days of K-K Barney Hogan. Jacob the baseball lover was of course among the exceptions.

But Jacob had a connection to Barney that went beyond baseball. Barney was the devoted friend of Jacob's cousin Buddy, for whom Jacob was waiting now—a lunch date.

The Barney and Buddy act—the former's half-embarrassed term for it—had begun under dramatic circumstances some five years earlier. Anticipating a traffic light change by a critical millisecond, Buddy had stepped off a kerb into the path of a taxi in a hurry. No possibility the cab could have stopped in time. No choice for Barney, though a perfect stranger then, to do anything but throw a shoulder at her, knocking her backwards out of the way. He himself made it only partially. The cab clipped his ankle, fracturing it in two places. Buddy tore her dress and lost an

inexpensive pair of sunglasses down a sewer. Thus, a clear
disproportion existed between them in terms of injury. In
the curious way these things sometimes work out, however,
it was Barney who, from that moment on, regarded himself
as responsible for Buddy. Over the next few months she
became the daughter he'd never had. In turn she permitted
him to become the father she'd always wanted. Neither was
the kind to ever put into words what this relationship
meant but Jacob—and everyone else at all close to them—
understood its texture.

Sipping the coffee Barney had just poured for him, Jacob
examined the other's girth with disapproval. 'I don't know
how you do it,' he said after a moment.

'What?'

'Keep getting fatter. Every time I leave Philly thinking
you've reached fat max, I come back and see how wrong I
was.'

'Damn it, Jacob, cut that out.'

'You were on a low cholesterol diet. What happened?'

'Jesus, you sound just like Buddy. Yak-yak-yak. Diet-
diet-diet. Big deal, I'm fat. I'm comfortable fat. What's the
worst that can happen? I'll get a heart attack and die?
Cancer beats the hell out of that? Besides, you ain't no
shrinking violet either, my friend.'

Jacob felt hands over his eyes and heard a voice say,
'Jacob's not fat. He's a big man, but he's solid, not a tub of
lard like you.'

He covered the small hands with his large ones and then
stood to embrace his cousin. She'd been asleep when he'd
arrived at her apartment late the night before—letting
himself in with his own key—and so this was the first he'd
seen of her in almost three months. (A note under the
coffee-pot had arranged their rendezvous.) He decided he
was not pleased. Her small, pale face seemed to him all
eyes, and the shadows under them were dramatic. She
appeared tense. Her smile which was usually so brightening
had the fitfulness of something forced.

But she asked all the right questions—about his health, Helen's. He asked questions of his own, and finally the reporting of family matters reached a state of currency. In the process he had learned that his former wife was quite contented with her new husband.

Buddy grinned, a real one rocketing out of the past. 'Actually, Shirley's delirious.'

'Good.'

'And she told me to tell you she now forgives you down to your last itty-bitty sin.'

Jacob accepted absolution without demur, and as a reward got his cheek bussed.

'And so do I,' Buddy said.

'Wonderful.' Seizing the moment he asked, 'Does it follow you'll be nicer to Helen?'

Tinges of colour appeared. 'Yes,' she said. 'I promise. You mean she still gives a shit?'

He knuckled her chin gently. 'Hey, hey, what is it with you?'

'Sorry,' she said. 'You know me and self-pity. If I don't wallow in it every so often I get the shakes.' Thumping the mahogany to attract Barney's attention: 'Barkeep, to me, please.'

He poured coffee for her, too, and delivered it.

'Jacob, you do look grand,' Buddy said. 'Doesn't he, Barney? That woman of his must know what it's all about.'

'Helen's class. Only female I ever met who could recite my career "K" total.'

'See? That's how you tell. Jacob, I want to hear about the tournament. When do you take on your first grand master?'

He replied that he was scheduled for his opening game the following afternoon, that he didn't yet know who the opponent would be, but that grand masters had nothing to fear from him for the foreseeable future. He was surprised to see this information received as if it were significant.

'They're not going to let you play Kaganovich?' she asked.

Expression bland, voice carefully colourless. The effect of course was to make interest as vividly apparent as blood through a scratch. What was going on here Jacob wondered. He glanced at Barney for a bit of insight and got an unhelpful shrug in response.

'Let?' he said. 'My dear child, let doesn't enter into it. True, Kaganovich has been among the missing for a while, but he once beat the world champ, for God's sake. Buddy, baby, have a heart.'

She went into a silence. Accustomed to her silences he usually found them easy to read. Not so this one, but he figured it made sense to ask if she knew Kaganovich.

'He's been in here,' she said. 'He's a friend of Barney's.' And then, excusing herself for the sake of a phone call she had to make, she abruptly left them.

Jacob said, 'Is she kidding? Kaganovich has been in here?'

Barney nodded. 'He's as hipped on baseball as you or Helen. He brought this scorecard for me to autograph. My last game, against the Giants.'

'But he's a Russian.'

'Dmitri Kaganovich was born on Flatbush Avenue, Brooklyn, New York. Lived there till he was thirteen when his Commie parents dragged him off to the USSR, kicking and screaming. The Russkis always claimed he was Russki, but Dimmie never did.'

'Dimmie?'

'And now he's as red-blooded American as you and me. Not only an American citizen but as of last year married to the the daughter of an American capitalist. You didn't know any of this?'

'What American capitalist?'

'He builds office buildings and stuff. Big ones, out near Portland, Oregon. God, I feel like I'm talking to Rip Van Winkle.'

Actually Jacob's condition of ignorance was not quite

that extraordinary. His interest in chess had lain fallow for so many years, and over the past three it had been the game itself that had absorbed him—that, plus the emanations it gave off of his dead father. As for the game's current luminaries they had glowed only sporadically.

Barney spent the next five minutes or so bringing him reasonably up to date on Kaganovich. After his stunning defeat of Boris Tsarkov, until then the Soviet's number two player (ranked only behind the world champion), Kaganovich had gone inactive—incomprehensibly. No tournaments, no exhibitions, nothing. Not that he was difficult to find, that wasn't it at all—he was more visible than he'd ever been. Sunning himself on a Black Sea beach, among the brisk walkers in Red Square, reading *Pravda* on a park bench . . . but no chess, absolutely none. And then suddenly there was—to Russians—the appalling news that he had applied for emigration. Twice permission had been denied and then unexpectedly granted. Some said, snidely, that the explanation lay with Tsarkov, who had not been averse to seeing so formidable a rival out of the country. All this had been ten years ago.

Kaganovich's first western port of call had been Canada. Five years there doing this and that (still no chess) and then, three years ago, another emigration. This time to a small university town in northern California as a result of being offered an assistantship in Russian literature plus a modestly endowed Chair of Chess. It was there he had met Elaine Rowell.

'Who's she?'

Barney scowled at him. Prodded thus, Jacob's brain revved up a notch and supplied the information. 'The capitalist's daughter,' he said. 'She's nuts about Tolstoy, is she?'

'She's nuts about Kaganovich. Also, she's a chess freak, like you. In fact she's entered in that tournament you're here for.'

'Which bracket?'

'How the hell would I know?' Barney said, and left to serve a customer.

Jacob spent less time digesting Barney's information than he might have because he saw Buddy come out of the phone booth. She did not look his way. She left the bar hurriedly. He thought of following her but didn't. Since she could hardly have forgotten he was here it must be she didn't want him along, he decided. He did, however, on Barney's return report the flight to him.

'Something must have come up,' Barney said, sourly enough for Jacob to take note. Barney could be sour about almost anyone but not Buddy, reserving for her not merely a special tone, but a special set of rules.

After studying him a moment Jacob said, 'She seems a bit—'

'Strung out,' Barney said.

'What's going on?'

'Every time you ask her you get a big phoney smile and the same horseshit answer: nothing.'

'How *long* has it been going on?'

'Couple of weeks maybe.'

Jacob thought about this, then: 'Her health?'

But now Barney was reassuring. 'Physically, she's all right,' he said. 'I'd bet on it.' He rubbed hard at a cigarette burn that had defaced his bar top for at least five years. 'She is so goddam close-mouthed. If she won a Pulitzer the *Sentinel* would let a few of us in on it, but *she* wouldn't. Or if she inherited a million bucks it'd be a secret until the day she bought you a Mercedes, right?'

Jacob smiled, thinking back to his own case in point. For a wedding present she'd given them a Peter Sculthorpe watercolour. Vivid with the fiery colours of early autumn, it had thoroughly captivated them. It had been delivered unceremoniously by a brace of off-duty cops, who would identify themselves no further. No hints as to the sender. Knowing Buddy as he did, however, Jacob had made the educated guess. On two counts Helen had been unwilling at first to believe him: (1) the terrific cost, (2) Buddy's disapproval of their marriage, no less real for being tacit. Still, persuaded by Jacob, she had written, thanking Buddy. In response came a one-word message: 'Windfall.' Hollywood, they learned later, had taken an option on one of her books.

Buddy *was* an eccentric, Jacob was prepared to acknowledge. As a child she'd been a loner. The fourth in a chain of daughters born to busy doctor parents—he a surgeon; she a pediatrician—Buddy was the first not to be a blazing beauty. That sealed her fate. 'A plain face is a lost face in my brother's house,' Jacob's father had said once in a rare moment of anger.

It wasn't that her parents meant to shut Buddy out. They were not malicious, merely insensitive. It was just that what was happening to her siblings was so much more ... insistent. Beauty creates a din. It is clamorous, and, being so, accrues to itself a disproportionate amount of space and time. So Buddy stole from street vendors, got into fights, became something of a truant, and bid for attention in a variety of other offbeat ways. Suddenly she was a full-fledged tomboy, astonishing and infuriating parents and sisters by going out for Pop Warner football. She made her team, too. Fleet and tricky, she was an outstanding little tailback. It took a while, but public opinion finally collapsed before her unmistakable talent and mulish determination. Even her family got around to breathing normally in her cleated, shoulder-guarded and helmeted presence.

Once they did, however, the charm of her football persona became less compelling to her. Moreover, something truly substantive had come into her life. She had discovered she could write. In fact it was Jacob—thirty to her fifteen—who had been the conduit. Having recently convinced himself that he could not write in any way that mattered, he was rocked by a poem of hers that he found by accident. Crumpled and dirty, scrawled on half a brown paper shopping-bag, it had fallen unnoticed out of a sweatsuit pocket. On Loneliness, it was called. Only three stanzas but full of the kind of eloquence that had always eluded him. He had torn it in small pieces and then taken himself off to a local gym where he punished a punching-bag for his own inadequacies. Two hours later, resentment under control, he told her how good he thought she was and changed her life.

None of Buddy's novels had sold much beyond break-even, but all four had been critical successes. The first had helped her get that initial, low-level job on the *Sentinel*. Slowly the jobs had improved and now, in her early thirties, her daily column was a *Sentinel* staple. Buddy's brand of aggressive introspection had found an audience, not vast but devoted. Her readers loved the highly personal, chip-on-the-shoulder way she reacted to their world.

Struck by a thought, Jacob said, 'Is she working on something? You know how she gets when she's in the middle of a book and it's not going right.'

Barney looked doubtful.

'Hell, maybe she's in love,' Jacob said.

Barney answered a phone call. Returning, he said, 'Don't think I've ever seen Buddy in love, have you?'

'Once. She was a kid. Guy got killed in Nam.'

'She never told me.' He shrugged. 'Why am I not surprised?' After a moment he said, 'How would you score that thing she had with Farrington last year?'

Jacob scowled. 'As an aberration.'

'Love, she'd take that hard, wouldn't she?' Barney said.

And then both men were silent, contemplating ramifications and possibilities.

'Hell with it,' Barney said. 'Whatever it is, it'll either get better or it won't. What's with you and this chess caper?' You see yourself as king of the hill some day?'

'Don't be dumb.'

'Then what?'

'I haven't been here for a while, so it was an excuse for a junket. Also Helen had to be away . . .'

'Bull,' Barney said. 'I know you, Jacob. You hide it, but the fact is you're a grudge-nurser. My guess is you think you've had some kind of breakthrough. So you're itching to test it, find out if maybe you're good enough to get back at some of those chess club guys who've been beating your brains out. Like him, for instance, speaking of the devil.'

Jacob was already aware of the entrance.

For the most part Jacob had the big man's easy response to his environment. Never pushed around much himself, he seldom saw the need to push anyone else around, and as a consequence was not really the stuff of which haters are made. But there was a quality in Simon Farrington that drew a jungle response from him, a special, almost preternatural alertness. Now he felt Farrington's hand on his shoulder. It had an instant effect on his hackles. Before turning he lifted the hand by the sleeve from which it extended and restored it to its owner.

Farrington grinned.

Simon St John Farrington was in his late forties, Jacob's age. He was small and rail-thin with the kind of clever, lively face—wide at the cheekbones and narrow at the jaw—that furnished the first clue to his nickname: Foxy. He had the requisite red hair and reddish brown eyes, too, and of course the innate slyness. A flamboyant fox, he wore a beautifully tailored white tropical suit, open-necked yellow shirt, white straw hat, a cane, a monocle—the point being to proclaim how little interested he was in understatement.

Foppishness aside, Farrington's reputation as a journalist was impressive. In addition to the weekly 'Farrington on Chess', he did a daily 'Farrington on the Rialto', his influential business/politics column. His success derived from two main sources—one admirable, the other far less so. Farrington was a self-described 'work ethic man'. He simply put in more hours than most of his rivals were willing or even able to. Less laudably, he was a sneak and a snoop of formidable accomplishment. No keyhole was safe from him—or trash can, for that matter. Thus, it was seldom possible to bury bodies deeply enough to keep Farrington from disinterring them. In high places they had learned to be sensible of his existence, nervously on occasion. That gave him power. What increased it was the knowledge, universally shared, that he was as incorruptible as he was idiosyncratic.

For a short period last year he had been Buddy's beau, for an even shorter period her fiancé. 'Foxy's never boring,' she had told Jacob. 'He doesn't think or act the way anybody else does. He's an original. No, of course I'm not in love with him. But he is with me, head over heels. And I find that terribly exciting. Damn it, Jacob, don't you look at me that way. How do *you* know that's not enough?' One day after slipping his ring on her finger she had returned it. Her apologies had been unacceptable to Farrington. Her long letter—in which she attempted to establish how undeserving an object she was for such ardent devotion—was equally unavailing. Seven months after receiving it he had not yet spoken to her though their *Sentinel* offices adjoined.

Even if Buddy had never been born, however, Farrington would have made Jacob his enemy. Nor was Jacob truly surprised. From the first he had recognized the type—the little man who sees the big man in no other perspective than as a calculated insult, as an invitation to invidious comparison, and therefore as a challenge: cut Goliath down to size. Still, there was no doubt that natural antagonism had received a booster around the time of the broken engagement.

But Farrington did not ignore Jacob as he did Buddy. On the contrary. Whenever he bumped into him—at Barney's or the chess club—he went out of his way to lavish attention on him.

Now, beaming, he said, 'The reports are true. Jacob is once more among us. Hogan, a welcoming drink for the lieutenant.'

'No, thanks,' Jacob said to Barney, who hadn't budged anyway.

Farrington flicked at Jacob the mini-smile he reserved for

indemnifying nastiness. 'All prepped for the Capa, are you, big fella?'

'Yeah,' Jacob said. He glanced at his watch, getting ready to emulate his cousin and announce a pressing phone call.

'Crave your indulgence, Jacob,' Farrington said. 'Came looking for you specially, but I won't keep you long. Just long enough to bring you news you'll be delighted to hear. But first, do you know how many are entered in our category?'

Jacob kept silent. For one thing 'in our category' was in itself a disconcerting phrase, since Jacob's rating was a humble 1155, which placed him some 300 points below the exact middle of all those ranked by the United States Chess Federation. (Grand masters, the chess elite, lived far northwards of this, in those remote regions starting at about 2500.) Farrington was officially *unrated*, but that was because he had always refused to play in tournaments sanctioned by the USCF on the grounds that he disagreed with it philosophically. What the nature of this disagreement was he never stipulated. Some—his detractors—said it was a disagreement rooted solely in the USCF's refusal to name him editor of its official publication a dozen years or so ago when the opportunity had presented. Thus, in a manner of speaking, Farrington and Jacob did share the Under 1400 category. In reality, though, Farrington quite regularly beat players rated 1800 and above. But now Jacob waited for the *other* shoe to fall.

'Hundred and sixteen of us,' Farrington said. 'Of *us*, Jacob. You did know I was entered?'

And there it was—the kind of dismal, discouraging thump other shoes invariably delivered.

'Yes indeed. When I saw your name on the rolls I decided to break the habit of a lifetime. I expect you to feel honoured, sir.'

'Yeah, honoured.'

Farrington's eyes seemed to Jacob twin red dots of malice. 'Of course with a category that full and each entrant scheduled for only six games there was an excellent chance we might not get to play each other and that would've been a waste, wouldn't it?'

After a moment Jacob said, 'You fixed someone, didn't you, you little bastard.'

'Let's just put it that I called in a favour. All for you, Jacob. No way I was going to let you down. 'Long about the third or fourth round, I believe. After which I'll do you up for "Farrington on Chess". After which I'll tack the column to the club bulletin board, with appropriate additional comments on three-by-fives, of course.'

Farrington was famous for his three-by-fives. He carried them around the way others might worry beads, whipping them out to make a note or record a quote. Or sometimes simply a *pensée*. And then disbursing them indiscriminately, pushing them like religious tracts on those not swift enough to elude him. Long ago, Foxy Farrington had decided he was a wise man and that wisdom—his, along with certain of the like-minded—must be disseminated. He saw his three-by-fives as instruments in a great cause.

He gave one now to Jacob, who crumpled up the card and jammed it out of sight unread.

'Well, now, big fella, how does my news strike you?'

'I'll live,' Jacob said.

Reprise of smile. 'True, but you won't be happy.' Flourish with the hat. Deep cavalier's bow. And exit.

'Je-sus!' Barney said, grabbing for his atomizer. It took vigorous spraying to restore the atmosphere to its customary saloon salubriousness. 'What the hell is that stuff he uses, *Fox in Heat?*'

Jacob drained his cup and signalled for a refill.

'Why do you put up with that shit from him?' Barney asked.

'What's my alternative?'

'Tear his ears off?'

Jacob looked at his hands. They seemed to him huge, larger and more lethal even than usual. He had a sense of them as twitching for action. He stuffed them in his pockets. 'There's a certain disproportion in size,' he said dourly.

Barney set his coffee down. 'Is he right? Will it really bother you if he hangs the column on the club bulletin board?'

'Yeah.'

'A lot?'

'Enough.'

Barney wiped at the bar again. 'What does the card say?'

Jacob located it, read it, then showed it to Barney.

> He can run, but he can't hide.
>
> *Joseph Louis Barrow*
> *Heavyweight Champion of the World*

'The little prick,' Barney said.

A brace of new customers drew his attention—and Jacob's too, because suddenly he recognized one of them, a cop like himself: Gene D'Agostino, Philadelphia homicide. Ten years ago they had worked together as part of an ad hoc squad on loan to the NYPD. A strangler, Jacob recalled vividly. A serial killer who had hanged himself—fitting end—when he sensed his pursuers closing in. D'Agostino saw him, concentrated, placed him, and started over, smiling.

They shook hands, saying the obligatory things to each other about time's restraint. In D'Agostino's case, Jacob thought it was true. Certainly he was better-looking in his late forties than he had given promise of being. In his thirties he had carried a low-slung paunch. Reversing the usual order of things, it was gone now. And he was much better dressed—white shirt, solid blue tie, faultless summer-weight pinstripes. He was also carefully if not stylishly coiffed and owned a well-tended blond moustache curled to natty points. Jacob, having seen such symptomatology before, made a diagnosis he'd have been willing to back for money:

ambition. D'Agostino, he felt, had sniffed the higher reaches and now yearned to be there. Too bad.

Nostalgically, they dredged up the final days of the strangler. Then they spent a few moments on autobiography—both were now lieutenants, Jacob in grade somewhat longer than D'Agostino. Having elicited this information, D'Agostino shifted tactfully. What was Jacob doing in Philly? Jacob explained about the chess tournament. D'Agostino took this in stride, helped, perhaps, by his having been introduced to Kaganovich the last time he had dropped into Barney's.

'Nice enough sort of guy,' he said, half turning to Barney, inviting him to agree. 'But kind of eerie.'

'Eerie?'

'No accent,' D'Agostino said. 'Sounds just like one of us. That's eerie for a Russian.'

'Brooklyn, New York,' Barney said. 'How come you can't get that through your thick cop's skull?'

'That's *his* story,' D'Agostino said.

Barney sighed heavily before moving off to see what thirsts were in need of slaking.

'Barney loves the man,' D'Agostino said to Jacob, but with the clear intention of being overheard. 'Barney'd love an axe-murderer who could remember his "K" total.'

Barney delivered a finger to D'Agostino and refills on the far fringe of the bar.

D'Agostino's eye caught the eye of the short, grey-haired personage with whom he had entered. This man had a very large jaw, a soldierly back, and a face not given to smiling. His fingers had now begun to drum some non-harmonious rhythm atop the bar.

'My captain,' D'Agostino said. 'Lipscombe. Want to meet him?'

It was the kind of invitation that contained in it an invitation to decline, and Jacob did so.

'Smart,' D'Agostino said. 'He wouldn't like you. But

that's OK—he doesn't like anybody. In particular, he doesn't like me. He thinks I want his job.'

'Do you?'

D'Agostino's face went blank, became for an instant the face of some totemic carving. When he spoke the tone matched. 'Actually, I want him dead. Then I want his job.'

It was as if he'd forgotten he wasn't alone. Jacob cleared his throat.

D'Agostino grinned. 'Now why the hell did I go and say a thing like that?'

'Probably because it's true,' Jacob said.

'Since when is that a reason?'

Jacob had no ready answer and kept silent.

They shook hands, promising to make a better effort to stay in touch this time, knowing they wouldn't. But before he left D'Agostino said, 'Read about your cases, you know. Impressed as hell.'

'Thanks,' Jacob said.

D'Agostino gave him a friendly pat on the shoulder. 'Draw two over there, Russki-lover,' he said to Barney and returned to duty.

CHAPTER 3

Shaky hands, bloodshot eyes, unshaven cheeks . . . and so on down the boozy inventory. Still, anyone else you might say bad night and let it go at that. But not this man, Helen thought. This was a man for whom the phrase bandbox smart had always seemed freshly minted. Tall, erect, gut in, gaze clear and commanding—that was the way George Adams customarily faced his world. And the way he'd been facing it not two months earlier when she'd tracked down a tricky case of office embezzlement for him.

'What the hell's wrong with you?' she asked, too taken aback for diplomacy.

It seemed to require a long time for him to focus on her, but when at last he did he waved her to the armchair on the other side of his desk. He kept silent, however. He continued to stare at what he'd been staring at when she entered, which, as far as she could see, was nothing.

She'd been in his study before. It was, in fact, one of her favourite all-time rooms—booklined and spacious. Thickrugged and leathery. Handsomely appointed but without any of the signs of 'rich man's opulence' that could so easily have marred it. It was the kind of room in which she had always felt private, and—she admitted—privileged. But right now it reflected the change in its owner. That is, it looked untended, cluttered. Butts in the ashtrays to overflowing; the smell of neglect unpleasantly pervasive. She knew beyond question that George's highly efficient staff of domestics had been forbidden the premises.

He shoved a bottle of Scotch towards her, and she shoved it back.

'I asked you a question,' she said.

'Haven't been sleeping too well,' he said.

'And you've been hitting that thing like it's going out of style, haven't you?' She indicated the bottle.

He shrugged. Heisting it, he was about to take another swig when she said, 'Do that, and I'm out of here.'

For a moment the bottle remained as delicately balanced as the course of events. Another millimetre and liquid would have to yield to the laws of physics, but in the meantime it remained poised precariously. Helen meant what she'd said. There had been too many drunks in her family for her to delude herself about them. You couldn't do business with them, and that was all there was to it. The question was, did he believe her. He did. He righted the bottle and guided its slow descent to the desk.

'OK,' she said, 'now talk sense.'

'What time is it?'

She told him.

'I've been in here going on thirty-six hours, drinking fairly steadily.'

'Bully for you,' she said.

'So why am I not drunk?'

'Metabolism.'

'What?'

'I'm waiting, George.'

Tilting his head, he squinted at her in a way that suggested he might be drunker than he thought. But there was no evidence of slurring when he said, 'You have off-spring, don't you?'

'Yes.'

'Yes, sure you do. A son. Lucky.'

'George, no bull—it's time to stop playing around. Give. Have you heard from the kidnappers?'

He laughed mirthlessly. 'Singular.'

'What's that supposed to mean?'

'Singular means one. One kidnapper. One victim. One person.'

After a moment Helen said, 'Deirdre kidnapped herself?'

He got up and a bit unsteadily crossed the room to the heavy, sound-proofing curtains, opening them. A sweep of lush green lawn was revealed, at the end of which you could see just the beginnings of an ample, kidney-shaped swimming pool. Lovely to be in it, Helen thought frivolously before discipline could be enforced.

'Did I ever tell you about John Gow?' he asked.

She shook her head. But then she said, 'Fielding's father?'

'Yes. He is—was—the genius who invented the V-gear.'

'Should I know what that is?'

'Do you have some kind of advanced engineering degree you haven't told me about?'

'No.'

'Well, then, the V-gear is—' He broke off, put a finger to his lips and looked about him with exaggerated concern. He beckoned her to come closer. She didn't, but he continued anyway. 'The V-gear is what we called it affectionately. It

has another name, of course, but for security reasons . . .
very hush-hush. OK?'

'OK.'

'The good old V-gear is a beautifully conceived and
designed piece of electronic wizardry shaped as you might
imagine. Micro-sized . . . so, so tiny. It goes into things, a
variety of things, many of which are used to make war. John
invented it, and I capitalized and then marketed it. We
were partners.'

'This really does have a bearing on why I'm here?'

He nodded. 'You'll see. Permit me to say, parenthetically,
that it also has a good many industrial applications—
peacetime applications, that is. But it's the military potential
that got us started. In 1966 John and I won a defence
contract that began our fortunes. Did I say we were partners?'

'Yes.'

'Did I also say we were friends? Not only partners, you
understand, but comrades in arms and close enough as
friends to be mistaken for brothers? Did I tell you that?'

'No.'

'Well, I'm telling you now. It's the booze of course that's
making it possible.' He paused. 'You're the first. Others
know the facts, naturally, but you're the first I've spoken to
about it. A signal honour.'

'Go on.'

He looked at her. The smile that thinned his mouth and
made it hard didn't last long, only long enough to clue her
in. But she waited for *him* to say it.

'Eight years ago he deserted his wife to run off with mine.'

Phlegmatically, then, he added details, none of which
really mattered.

When he was finished he waited for her to comment, but
she didn't. There was nothing she could think of at the
moment that would have been serviceable. He reached for
the bottle again and this time she didn't stop him. She let
her breath out heavily, slumped in her chair, and thought

once more that lush, green swimming pools were made for days like this. Such a *cheerful* shade of green. Such a pleasant sense of palpability to the water. He pillowed his head on his arms. She sat with him until he fell asleep, and then she went into the house proper to see if there was someone around who could help her find Deirdre.

CHAPTER 4

Stripped of the social engagement that would have occupied the early part of the afternoon, Jacob found himself at loose ends. The tournament didn't get under way until tomorrow. He could do some additional studying, he supposed—review the various Sicilian defences he'd be counting on heavily, for instance—but he knew that wouldn't be really useful. Too much like last-minute exam cramming. He sauntered along Broad Street for a while, stopping here and there to watch it being torn up. Jacob was fond of Philadelphia. Not only was it his birthplace, but it was where he had spent the early, happy years of his first marriage. As with most big cities, however, it was not at its best when viewed casually. You had to live in a city, Jacob knew, in order to hear its music. Like an experienced woman, Philadelphia played it safe with strangers. Bare-backed construction workers hovered over a hole in the ground, but their approach to widening it was too desultory to sustain interest. Jacob did not attach blame to that. It was a sweltering day in early July, temperature and humidity suddenly skyrocketing after a spell of unseasonal balminess. How hot was it? Hot enough to get the hell out of it. Screw Foxy Farrington, Jacob decided, and made for the Quaker Chess Club as if it were an oasis. If Farrington had preceded him Jacob would coolly grin and bear it, coolly the operative word.

The building was shabby enough to suggest that its

history might be interesting. It wasn't. It was merely a relatively new building that had gone to seed fast. The rent was predictably cheap. An ambulance-chasing lawyer, a small-time accountant, and an employment agency for domestic help were its star tenants. Quaker Chess, with its modest membership roll—80 thereabouts—felt right at home.

Jacob stepped out of the arthritic elevator on the fourth (and top) floor. He pushed open the heavy door, and in the tiny ante-room saw at once that Teddy Sherman and the ancient doctor who was his arch enemy were, as ever, locked in combat. Teddy was the club caretaker, about 75, whose style of play was ferocious. The doctor, about 80, was if anything even more aggressive. In fact both old men moved pieces so quickly that sometimes—watch intently as he might—it was hard for Jacob to assess positions since they changed so rapidly.

As Jacob entered he heard Teddy's raspy voice in its habitual complaint to the chess gods. 'Man's too good for me. Look at him, a friggin' machine. How about a mistake, Krueger? One lousy mistake. Is that too much to ask?'

'Come on, come on,' Doc Krueger said. 'You're a piece ahead. You're everything ahead. Stop complaining and move already.'

Jacob grinned. It could have been yesterday, not three months ago, that he'd been here last.

'Don't know why I sit down with the *momser*', Teddy said and attacked violently with a rook that almost instantly found itself beleaguered.

'Check, if you don't mind.' Doc Krueger's voice had become unctuously apologetic now that he was closing in for the kill. Two moves later an enraged Teddy knocked his king down in token of defeat and paid the quarter that made it binding.

Both oldsters had been well aware of Jacob's presence, but neither spoke until the issue between them was decided. Nor had Jacob expected them to. Chess players, a diverse enough breed, all had that much in common: the game first, civilities a distant second.

Teddy—tiny and frail with unkempt white hair and the sharp stare of a former high-roller—allowed himself to smile welcomingly now. 'Jacob, where you been? I could have been dead you stayed away so long.'

'Dead? You? You'll outlive me by fifty years. And Doc Krueger will outlive us both.'

The doctor dissolved in laughter.

'Foxy was around this morning looking for you,' Teddy said.

'He found me.'

'Sure he did. Krueger here couldn't keep his mouth shut and told him try Barney's.'

'He needed me to tell him that?' Doc Krueger demanded defensively. 'Since when don't the whole world know when Jacob's in town, try Barney's for him. I did wrong, Jacob?'

Jacob patted the old man's shoulder.

Teddy was studying him. 'You're entered in the Capa, I hear. Why?'

Jacob shrugged. 'Something to tell my grandchildren.'

'Wrong, bubby. I think it's because you like punishment. All right, there's a babyface in the back room waiting for you.'

'What kind of a babyface?'

'With mean eyes.'

'Let him wait. I didn't come to Philly to be hustled by one of your babyfaces.'

'Nah! Nah! He don't hustle yet. Next year maybe. Go, Jacob. I'll yak to you later. Right now, the doctor wants another piece of me. Look, he's slobbering.'

The gleeful doctor bounced a bit in demonstration.

As he moved off towards the back room, Jacob heard Teddy trying to get a knight as a handicap. Moans and groans on behalf of the effort, but Jacob knew the doc was too canny. Still, Teddy might talk a pawn out of him. If he could, he might well get his quarter back.

Quaker Chess was laid out like an archetypal railroad flat—four rooms one after the other. Nothing seedy about its interior, however. Not plush either, but the walls were freshly painted white and the photos of club members— a handful of them quite well known—were respectfully arranged and dust free. Teddy did look after things. Depending on its size, each room had six to eight chessboards set up. Players for them were still sparse, though in about half an hour they would not be. By then, around noon, as many as 20 would probably be in attendance, while by day's end an average of 60 would have passed through.

The babyface in the back room might or might not have been mean-eyed, but he was certainly tender in years. Jacob guessed about 13. He was thin and very black. Bent over the current issue of *Chess Life*, he was so deep in a problem that an army of Jacobs would not have claimed his full attention. As he lifted his head, blinking, he looked like a cranky old owl encountering sudden daylight. Jacob identified himself, held out a hand in greeting. It was shaken absently. The problem was still much more with him than Jacob was, large as Jacob was.

'Want a game?' Jacob asked politely.

The invitation was taken under advisement. 'Do you have a rating?'

Jacob announced it and watched as his fate hung in the balance. Perhaps because there was no one else in the room, no witness to this stepping down in class, Babyface decided in his favour.

'Mine's 58 points higher,' he said, 'but all right, I'll play you. Sometimes I don't mind playing patzers. I get a chance to try things.'

Instantly then he reached for the white pieces—and their inherent advantage—to set them up on his side of the board. Try things, my ass, Jacob thought. The kid's a born chess player. The only vein he knows is the jugular.

But Babyface was merely OK, not the *Wunderkind* he thought himself. Soon enough Jacob was a pawn up with potential developing for a bruising kingside attack. Babyface was not happy.

'You lied about your rating,' he said. 'You lowered it, so you could sandbag me.'

'Nary a point,' Jacob said.

It was then they heard a stirring in the front room—Teddy's distinctive rasp a decibel or so above other raised voices. It took a moment to be reassured that the clamour was essentially benign. Jacob had risen to investigate. So, too, had his opponent, who managed to knock the board over in the process. Jacob stared at him. He stared back.

'Sure am one clumsy Robert,' he said blandly.

'Yeah,' Jacob said. 'Start over?'

'No way,' clumsy Robert said. 'I don't play with no sandbaggers.'

He strolled nonchalantly out of the room.

Impressed, Jacob watched after him. If he survives to fifteen, he told himself, he may make champion.

By now it was clear the raised voices signified excitement and welcome. Teddy was sounding a clarion call. 'Hey, look who's here—friggin' Dimmie Kaganovich.'

The room just at the head of the skinny corridor was the club's largest, and, after replacing the scattered pieces, Jacob worked his way towards it. He heard a burst of laughter and arrived as a second, larger burst detonated. Jacob had no trouble identifying Kaganovich. He was poised over a board, moving chessmen with a kind of negligent grace—not really moving them, just sort of flicking at them. As a result they didn't quite fill the squares they were aimed at, but young Robert, exuding amiability now, was there to do the neatening up. Kaganovich was slim, good-looking, and expensively dressed. Jacob, no men's wear model, nevertheless knew he'd be right to put high figures on the smooth linen shirt with initials discreetly embroidered on the pocket, the well-cut worsted trousers, and the gorgeous tasselled loafers. He had thick, black, curly hair, and high cheekbones, testament to the Slav in him. His skin was dark, not sun-tanned, but gipsy-dark, as were his eyes—dark and almost violently expressive. At first glance Jacob thought early thirties, revising this upward on closer inspection. There was something sad, even harrowed, about those dark, expressive eyes. Still, it was clear that just then at least he was enjoying himself. In turn his audience— of two dozen or so—was finding him irresistible.

As Jacob entered Kaganovich was replaying his climactic game against Boris Tsarkov, the one preceding his defection. Even Jacob knew the bare bones of that story, at least the *Chess Life* version, but the version Kaganovich was in the midst of was a lot livelier. It was unorthodox, outrageous, and, Jacob felt, improvised as well. In fact Kaganovich seemed to be surprising—and delighting—not only his audience with its twists and turns but himself even more so.

Suddenly, as if it were a pinch of salt, Kaganovich dropped the black king over his shoulder. 'And just like that I had him,' he said in the American English so unsettling to D'Agostino. 'Why? Tell me why.' A variety of suggestions were put forward. 'No, sir. No, no, and hell no. I had him because he's Boris and I'm Dimmie, and I know him better than anyone else in the whole world. Better than his mother. Better than any broad he ever slept with, not that there have been all that many. And I knew Capablanca was in his mind. You heard me, Capa! Remember Capa versus Menchik, what Capa said about the trap he sprung? He said my opponent should have considered that a player of my experience and strength would never have made such a move if it were really that inviting. So I *knew* I could leave that bishop hanging for at least one more shot. Anyone else, Boris would have grabbed it. Me, he didn't dare. Because every contest we'd ever had he lost to me. Chess, girls, soccer, spelling bees, for God's sake. He was spooked, is what I'm telling you. Convinced by history that he was staring into a trap, he let the bishop go, and that gave me the time I needed to set up queenside and smash him.

After that he was so shaken he lost two straight to Cyril Cunningham, that in and out Brit he'd never lost to before or since, and kissed goodbye his shot at the world championship that year. Maybe forever. Because the next time he looked around there were Karpov and Kasparov.'

'And he's never forgiven you,' someone said.

Kaganovich grinned. 'You noticed.'

Other questions and comments followed, and the next ten minutes featured an animated give and take between Kaganovich and his audience. It was a representative Quaker Club turn-out, Jacob thought, which meant a variety of ages, colours, and social classes. He recognized a couple of lawyers, a cop, an accountant, an advertising copywriter, and a reformed alcoholic with a penchant for becoming unreformed (and unglued) whenever he entered a tournament. There was also a sporting goods salesman, and a fat, fortyish dock-worker who some said was 'family-connected'. And of course there were Teddy (beaming, reflecting the glow of a great occasion), Doc Krueger, and, conspicuously, young Robert. No females, however. Women were still relatively exotic in the world of chess, and the Quaker Club membership reflected this. Two belonged, Jacob knew, though he'd never seen either of them.

Demographically diverse, the Quaker Clubbers were uniformly savvy about chess, and the questions aimed at Kaganovich gave him ample opportunity to be wittily irreverent at the expense of Tsarkov and other Russians, the American chess establishment, the murky politics of international chess, and, most charmingly, at his own expense. Then someone suggested an impromptu simul— Kaganovich against six boards. He hesitated and seemed, for some reason, to send a glance Jacob's way, but after a moment agreed. The boards were set up. Jacob watched for a bit, saw without regret that Kaganovich was going to crush young Robert, whereupon, nudged by a certain gnawing in his stomach, he decided to go to lunch. He kissed the bald spot atop Teddy's head and left.

The elevator had lurched to three on its way down when the club door opened. It was Kaganovich.

'Good,' he said. 'I caught you. You're Jacob Horowitz, aren't you?'

Jacob acknowledged that he was.

'Barney guessed you might be here. I need to talk to you.'

'Sure,' Jacob said.

Kaganovich gestured towards the club. 'Got myself into something I hadn't intended to.' Rueful grin. 'Story of my life. About half an hour, I figure.'

Jacob nodded.

'Hey, have you had lunch? No? Good. We'll have it together, OK? Pick a place.'

Jacob named a restaurant frequented by Quaker Club members and told Kaganovich how to get there, after it was agreed that Jacob should go on ahead and book a table. Jacob hit the elevator button once more, but Kaganovich did not immediately return to the club. Jacob looked at him. The Kaganovich smile was charmingly in place.

'The thing is,' he said, 'someone wants to kill me. And I'm damned if I know what to do about it.'

With that as his exit line he opened and then shut the door behind him. Jacob thought of following but decided there wasn't much he could accomplish in that crowded club. The elevator finally arrived again, and he got in it. He would go to the restaurant and wait. He waited a long time. When the complaints of his stomach became clamorous he lunched—alone. Later he called the Dunsany, the hotel where the tournament was being held and where most of the out of town players usually stayed. Mr Kaganovich was not in his room, the desk clerk told him, adding that he had not long ago crossed the lobby with a young woman. They were heading towards the coffee shop. Jacob decided it was just his day for getting stood up.

CHAPTER 5

'On the chess board lies and hypocrisy do not survive long,' Emmanuel Lasker said and Jacob thought that was true. He looked up from the book. Yes, even in his own limited experience he had seen flashy, jerry-built attacks founder before defences established on righteous principles. He returned to Lasker, permitting the venerable grand master to enlarge on his theme. 'Many a man, struck by injustice as, say, Socrates and Shakespeare were struck, has found justice realized on the chess board and thereby recovered his courage.'

The phone rang while Jacob was savouring this. Helen. He told her about Lasker. She said she missed both of them. Then she said, 'I want to read *you* something. It's very short, and the words are cut out of newspapers. OK?'

'Shoot.'

'"Your daughter Deirdre is being held until you agree to negotiate." That's it.'

'Negotiate what?'

She took a moment before answering. 'Let me back up a bit. Do you remember Fielding Gow?'

'Yeah. A hard-nose.'

'But likeable.'

Jacob agreed, with reservations. He recalled a young man barely twenty—he'd be twenty-five now—extravagantly good-looking and exceedingly well-heeled. He also recalled an over-aggressive manner that could set teeth on edge at first meeting. Maybe even on second or third meetings, until somehow you became aware of how much raw insecurity was being camouflaged. Helen now added details to Gow's biography. At the age of sixteen he had inherited an impressive hunk of Illinois real estate, plus a thriving Mid-Western cattle bank, plus a reasonably profitable New England shoe factory, plus a substantial interest in something called the V-gear (which Helen promised to elaborate on later if Jacob wished her to). On paper he was worth upwards of ten million. Paradoxically, his sense of self-worth was negligible. And so he drank, caroused, gambled, consorted with hucksters and hustlers, and got into minor scrapes with the law. And then there would be periods—apparently he was in one such now—when he wouldn't touch his money; when, in consequence, he dropped out of sight and into some disreputable south Chicago fleabag. He never said why, but to Helen it felt right to view those as hair-shirt times, exercises in mortification. At any rate none of this was behaviour calculated to reassure a prospective father-in-law, particularly one as intellectually and emotionally committed to success as George Adams was, an achiever from birth. And then of course there were Fielding's genealogical difficulties. She set them in their proper context.

'But George backs and fills about that,' Helen said, wrapping up. 'I mean, for instance, whenever I nominate heredity as flat out pivotal he sort of shrugs it off, insisting on Fielding's character flaws as the source of his, George's, major concern. And never mind what he said when liquored up.'

'Lies and hypocrisy,' Jacob said, mostly under his breath.

'What?'

'How did Gow die?'

'Why?'

'Just wondered.'

'Once a homicide cop, always a homicide cop,' she said. 'It was an automobile accident.' She paused. 'The fact of the matter is I wondered, too, and made some calls. There's a view that holds it was mission accomplished. A state cop clocked him at over a hundred.'

'Drunk?'

'Apparently not.'

'How about the women?'

'Dead, too. Mrs Adams—who became Mrs Gow a year

or so after she left George—in childbirth. Some improbable thing having to do with a freaked out umbilical cord. Killed the baby also. God, Jacob, life can get—' She broke off, took a moment to regroup and continued. 'In the same month Mrs Gow—that is, Fielding's mother—fell off a polo pony. Broke her neck.'

Jacob grunted his own response to the ruthlessness with which life could clear a stage.

They were silent for a while and then Jacob said, 'So this private cold war's been going on for, what, seven, eight years now?'

'Not so cold. Not with Deirdre on hand. She's been nuts about Fielding since forever. Crazy about him when they used to swap lunch-boxes at Miss Faulkner's Country Day School, adored him as a preppie football hero, and through all those other phases, too, the downers as well as the uppers. It can get pretty bitter between the Adamses over Fielding Gow, despite the fact that they really do love each other a lot. Anyway, George wins a skirmish every now and then, but home comes Deirdre from Switzerland or the Riviera or London or whatever seductive place he's sent her in the hope of distraction, and soon enough the battle's resumed. Pretty hot at the moment, I'd say. Lot of different words might describe George Adams right now, but smouldering is one of them.'

'I didn't think he knew how to smoulder,' Jacob said and waited for her to comment. When she didn't, he added, 'But I guess I'm wrong.'

'He's human, Jacob. As human as the rest of us.'

Not sure he welcomed the concept of a human George Adams to lay over the already established strata of rich, powerful, and attractive, he hurried on. 'OK, we're back to negotiate. It's Deirdre who wants to, right?'

She laughed. 'You got there fast, honey man. Well, that is the way it looks, doesn't it? At any rate George is convinced she's kidnapped herself, and I think that nails it. Nor do I think there was really much attempt to delude anyone about that. Why then cut words out of newspapers? One possible explanation has to do with Deirdre being Deirdre. She rather marches to a different drummer.'

'So what does Adams really want from you?' Keeping his voice carefully uninflected.

'A miracle, I guess.'

Jacob was silent, thinking his own thoughts about what might or might not constitute a miracle in Adams's terms.

'What George wants me to do is weave a spell, as a result of which Deirdre will be delighted to come home and never see Fielding Gow again as long as she lives, knowing that hooking up with him would be tantamount to wrecking her life since he's obviously such a disaster.'

'That's all?'

'I can't think of anything else.'

'Why don't you say—piss off, George. This is no job for a PI.'

'I could do that, couldn't I?'

'But you won't.'

'George points out that Deirdre trusts me. Not only does Deirdre trust me, but for some reason Fielding does, too, and that makes me unique. I'm going to wait around a bit, Jacob.'

'For what?'

'For a call. And then we'll see. OK?'

Not having much choice—but not very obligingly either—he said, 'OK.'

There was a moment of rather charged silence.

'Jacob, it looks to me as if two kids I like might be in deep trouble. I don't want to turn my back on them. If I did I'd feel rotten about it.'

'And it looks to me as if maybe somebody's selling you a bill of goods.'

'If you're right and I'm wrong I won't waste a minute shaking loose. OK?'

He was a little better at it this time. 'OK,' he said.

Then he told her that Buddy might also be a seeker after help and fleshed that out a bit. Next, he ran down the collateral events of the day with particular reference to those surrounding Kaganovich.

'Someone wants to kill me,' she echoed musingly. 'I don't suppose that could be a manner of speaking? Chess players have a way of talking in metaphor, don't they? There *is* something murderous about that game.'

Jacob thought about it a moment. 'No, I'd say he was scared. More than he showed.'

'All right, so why the jilt?'

'Back to back jilts,' Jacob said, bathed in bathos.

She laughed. 'Poor Jacob.' For remedy she told him how empty her hotel room felt without him, dwelling with picturesque emphasis on the matter of the large double bed which she was about to occupy with her lonely self. (And how it seemed to yearn for a bearish bulk.) She was persuasive. After a while they said affectionate good nights to each other.

Jacob had just retrieved Lasker when he heard Buddy's key in the door.

'Place is a mess,' she said. Her glance was uneasy but defiant, the glance of someone who has made up her mind to attack at all costs. She disappeared almost at once into the kitchen.

He sent his own glance surveying the spacious living-room of the generous-sized apartment. It *was* a mess, but the pantyhose, sweaters, shoes and peach nightgown did not belong to him. Neither did the strewn-about books, magazines and newspapers. There were two bedrooms. Jacob's mess was confined to the smaller of the two and was a mess only in the most expansive sense of the word. He began to think positively about gathering it up and moving it to the Dunsany.

Some of this might have shown in his face because on emerging from the kitchen with a glass of milk, she took one look, put the glass down, sank on to the sofa and began to cry. Buddy, crying, was not an everyday sight. Jacob went to her, took her in his arms, and made crooning noises. She cried hard for some little time. People not used to crying don't stop easily, Jacob thought. Nor do they seem to get that much relief from it. But at last she was quiet, so much so he thought she might have gone to sleep.

'Buddy?'

She made a responsive noise, then sat up, face tear-blotched.

'So talk to me,' he said.

'I can't.'

'Why not?'

'It's too damn silly, and I'm ashamed of myself. And I hate the thought of you ashamed of me, too.'

'That'll be the day.'

'Jacob, I'm sorry about lunch today.'

Before he could answer, the doorbell rang. Jacob looked at his watch—a few minutes past eleven. Not the most conventional hour for a visit, but there was no point in delivering his lecture on not admitting callers who hadn't adequately identified themselves. One, she already had the door open. Two, he was suddenly convinced she had known perfectly well who would be on the other side. But it surprised him, all right: Kaganovich. Had he tracked him down at this hour because he, too, wished to apologize? A wild thought. In the next instant Jacob understood how little he had to do with Kaganovich's visit.

'Come,' Kaganovich said, reaching for Buddy's hand.

She snatched it away.

He managed to reclaim it and was dragging her to the door. 'Damn it, Buddy, I won't stand for any more of this. We have got to talk this out.'

By this time Jacob, seeing no alternative, was on his feet, preparing to deal himself in. He needn't have bothered. The crack Buddy's freed hand made against Kaganovich's unprotected cheek spoke volumes for the women's movement.

'Bitch,' Kaganovich said and shot a glance at Jacob. It was full of fury, though Jacob knew he need not take it personally. At that moment he meant no more to Kaganovich than the coat-rack he toppled, staggering back from Buddy's wallop.

Kaganovich slammed the door and was gone.

An instant later so was Buddy, the door to her bedroom slamming similarly.

Jacob was left alone, thinking that if Helen were there she might be able to suggest something constructive in the way of a next step. He tried to imagine what that might be. Nothing he could place confidence in came to mind, but he knocked at Buddy's door anyway.

'Please, Jacob, let me alone. I'm perfectly all right. Go to bed or something. I'll see you in the morning.'

Though her voice was reasonably steady he recognized 'perfectly all right' as flagrant overstatement. Still, short of kicking her door in, he did not see what he could do about it. He paced the apartment for a while, then decided his restlessness needed more scope.

Emerging from the building, he heard his name called— Kaganovich, from a darkened doorway across the street.

'I was just going to phone you, ask you to come out,' he said, hurrying to catch up.

Jacob kept walking.

'You're sore at me, right? How long did you wait?'

'Three days.'

'Honest to God, I had no choice.'

'OK,' Jacob said.

'And there was no way I could get to a phone. It was Buddy, you see. First she said she wouldn't meet me. Then, suddenly she changes her mind and says she will. And I was afraid if I . . . Look, my car's just around the corner. It's a terrific car, a beautiful car. How about if we take it out on the highway for a while?' And when Jacob hesitated: 'Please, one chess player to another.'

Jacob surrendered. Such an anointment was irresistible.

It *was* a terrific car, though not the flashy BMW sports model he had half expected. Instead it was an elegant navy blue Jaguar, an XJ6. The feel and smell of quality wiped Jacob's face like a towel when he opened the door. Silently, it got under way. Its driver, too, was silent until they had crossed the bridge into Camden and were on Route 130 leading to the Turnpike.

'Yeah,' Kaganovich said then, a long luxurious drawl. 'Always wanted a baby like this. Expensive but well short of gaudy. Oh, if my father could see me now.'

'He'd be proud of you?'

Kaganovich grinned.

'Not proud? He'd envy you?'

'He'd turn over in his grave. So would my mother. They were people of principle. Poor but principled. Every month or so they'd have little "Dimmie is dead to us" ceremonies. My wife, on the other hand, has no principles. None whatever. She does, however, have a mission. It's to domesticate Dimmie. She thinks it'll help if she buys me things. She's right, of course. You owe her this ride, Jacob. Incidentally, do you know my wife?'

'No.'

He smiled enigmatically. 'And nobody else does either.'

Jacob, not in possession of the facts, said nothing.

Kaganovich gunned the motor and the car reacted as if it had huge muscles and was hungry for exercise. In seconds they were past 80 and climbing.

'Cut it out,' Jacob said. 'In case you've forgotten, I'm a cop.'

'Sorry,' Kaganovich said.

Uncomplainingly, the Jag decelerated to a decorous 65. When it had settled in there Kaganovich asked, 'Aren't you curious about Buddy and me?'

'I figure that's why we're out here. So you can enlighten. About that, and about the homicide in your life. That wasn't a joke, was it? Someone *is* threatening to kill you?'

Kaganovich lifted himself a bit so he could reach into his

trouser pocket for three crumpled pieces of paper. One by one he passed them to Jacob, then flicked on the overhead light. Death threats were like kidnap notes, Jacob decided, in that their contents were constructed out of newspapers:

1. Guilty! Prepare to pay for your sins.

2. Kaganovich, you are under sentence of execution.

3. Will it be the pellet? No. Will it be the rope? No. Will it be soon? Mother of God, yes!

Jacob looked up when he was finished reading and Kaganovich turned off the light. 'They arrived in that order—the third one only this evening, *after* I spoke to you at the chess club. I found it slipped under my door. The first two scared hell out of me. It's a damn funny feeling, having to say to yourself, Dimmie, you've got that kind of enemy.'

'The first two? Why not the third?'

'Because now I'm clued in to who sent them.'

'Who did?'

Kaganovich smiled as if at some private joke. Then he said, 'I wonder how much you know about the politics of power chess, Soviet style.'

'Not much,' Jacob said.

'Did you know that in the USSR great chess players are routinely asked to go into the tank if the situation seems right?'

'To whom?'

Kaganovich shrugged. After a moment he said, 'Chess in the Soviet Union is not like chess anywhere else. That is, it's a game only in the most superficial sense. What it is, really, is something the state uses to score propaganda victories. Think about that for a moment. Now take it to its logical conclusion. I mean, if Russian citizens demonstrate marked superiority over the citizens of other nations in an arena as brainy as chess, then there's an inference to be drawn. The Politburo likes that inference. It would do a lot to protect the status quo in which that inference seems viable. As a consequence it pays very close attention to developments and reputations. It *cares* what reputations are made, and if favourite sons can be glamourized from time to time with a stirring victory, why somebody's going to be asked to make less than all the right moves. Do you follow?'

'Is that what happened to you?'

Kaganovich nodded.

Jacob took a guess. 'It was the KGB that asked?'

Kaganovich hesitated but then nodded again.

'And you agreed?'

'Of course.'

'Of course,' Jacob echoed phlegmatically.

But then Kaganovich sighed. 'Alas, the fact is I double-crossed them.'

'Why?'

An eyebrow climbed but Kaganovich looked amused. 'The possibility that I might be honest never entered your mind?'

'I mean that the KGB is pretty heavy stuff to be messing around with, or so I gather.'

'You betcha. And I had every intention of being good as gold, only it seems I couldn't.' Kaganovich was silent a moment, recalling. 'There I was sitting at the chess board, and it was as if discretionary behaviour was no longer possible. I wanted to *win*. Let me rephrase that. I mean that the desire to win was—always is—so powerful I simply had no choice. I can't stand being beaten, Jacob. You think that's hyperbole, but it isn't. I get physically ill. I mean even now, just talking about it, I get this queasy feeling in my stomach.'

'But that's the breed, they tell me.'

Kaganovich nodded.

'My father was like that,' Jacob said.

'Your father was a hotshot?'

'A club player at his best, but good enough to have the bug.'

'The win-at-all-costs bug.'

'Yeah.'

Kaganovich smiled. 'In his little sixteenth-century book of advice and counsel, Ruy Lopez says—place your opponent with the sun in his eyes. Anyway, name *my* opponent that day, can you?'

'Tsarkov.'

'Yours in one. And so now you also know who sent me those so-called death threats.'

'So-called?'

'Oh hell, yes. Listen, at first I thought they were my father-in-law's bright idea, and that *did* worry me. A meaner, more vindictive son of a bitch doesn't walk this earth than Royal Rowell. Last year he paid a pair of goons to beat me up. I was lucky, somebody saw them in action and called the cops, but they still had time to crack two of my ribs. If it had been him I'd still be in a sweat. Or for that matter if it had been Lanie, my wife. Now Lanie's a good woman, I'd never say she isn't, but she *is* a Rowell. Moreover, she's very, very quiet. My experience with those quiet ones is that they tend towards unpredictable behaviour. Joan of Arc was a quiet woman. I bet you Bonnie of Bonnie and Clyde was, too. And the thing is, nobody could exactly blame her for damning Dimmie in her secret heart. And you know, even Buddy . . .' He rubbed his cheek pointedly. 'You understand what I'm saying? There are those who can explode given the right set of circumstances, and then there are the bull-shitting pop-offs like Boris, the original Russian teddy-bear.'

'What makes you so sure it *is* Tsarkov?'

'I'm sure, I'm sure. It's the eve of the big tournament, see, and what you're looking at is a peasant's version of psychological warfare. Enough, I want to talk about Buddy now, OK?'

'Go ahead.'

'Actually, it's a very short story. We met at Aspen. Last December, it was. December 2nd. At this ski lodge. We were both lots better as skiers than almost anyone else up there at the time, and so we were sort of thrown together. But the funny thing is how fast it happened. I'm checking in, she's coming out of an elevator. Click! By the third day we were talking about marriage, honest to God. I couldn't believe myself.' He paused. His eyes seemed at that moment not merely melancholy but haunted by an overview of his own personal history. 'And I didn't, really, if you want to know the truth. Anyway, home I go to begin the process known to my friends and intimates as Dimmie chickening out. Before year's end I wrote her.'

Fitting dates together, Jacob decided he might well have his first real insight into the Buddy–Farrington connection. Ol' Debbil Rebound, was his guess. Early in January Buddy had accepted, then rejected, Foxy's ring.

'OK, so you chickened out. And then?'

Kaganovich looked glum. 'Guess.'

'That's when you married the capitalist's daughter and lived happily ever after?'

'Not so happy as all that.'

'No?'

'For one thing, the capitalist won't quit. He's all over me all the time. He hasn't been able to scare me off, so every other day he tries some new dodge to make my life miserable. Like he's got flunkeys practically going door to door telling everybody in Portland I'm a fortune-hunter.'

'Fancy that.'

He struck sharply at the rim of the steering-wheel. 'And the other damn thing is I can't get Buddy out of my mind.'

'What a shame. Why don't you hang the next right, please, and get us off this.'

'That's it? You're satisfied? It's OK for me to trifle with Buddy's affections?'

'I'm not her keeper.'

'What do you mean—you're not. You *are*. God, the things she told me about her hero cousin. I mean, you're supposed to beat my brains out just for thinking erotic thoughts about her, and here all you've got to say is—I'm not Buddy's keeper.'

'You *want* me to beat up on you, is that it?' Then not waiting for an answer: 'Sure you do. Is that the way it always works with you? Something rotten, followed by a couple of therapeutic lumps and bruises. Modest, nothing major. But the decks are cleared for something rotten again?'

'Goddam parlour psychiatrists,' Kaganovich said, shuddering for emphasis. 'How I hate 'em.'

'Yeah,' Jacob said. 'I think we're beginning to grate on each other.'

Kaganovich made the suggested turn and for the next few minutes neither spoke. Then Jacob heard him laugh bitterly. 'Not that you're wrong,' he said. 'OK, now you know two important things about me. That I hate losing. And that when I'm naughty I crave punishment in order to get back in action. Remember them.'

'Why?'

'Who knows, maybe my biographer will ask you for a quote some day.'

'I doubt it,' Jacob said.

After a moment Kaganovich said, 'She's the first woman I ever really thought I might make it with. Long term, that is. I don't say I actually could have, of course. It's just that only with Buddy did the possibility ever occur. And, you know, I've been thinking it might be true of her, too. I mean, down deep you might be looking at a one-man woman. She won't admit that, hell, no. She says she hates me, and maybe a part of her does by now. But there's another part, a buried part, that isn't going to forget me. You have to understand that with Buddy there was never any question of a scam. I mean, she saw through me from the start, knew everything there is to know.'

'And what is there to know?'

'That I'm a no-goodnik. She liked me in spite of it.' He stole a glance sideways. 'And so do you. Yeah, Jacob, I got you figured out. You're one of those people drawn by no-goodniks. Which is pretty funny, seeing you're a cop. Or maybe it isn't.'

Jacob kept silent. Imperceptibly, the Jag had been asserting itself and had reached a startling 85 when he happened to catch sight of the gauge.

'Cut it,' he said. 'Right now, Buster, or so help me you'll spend time in the lock-up.'

Kaganovich grinned but obeyed. 'I owe myself 25 bucks,' he said. 'I bet you wouldn't notice until 90.'

'Or until you got us both killed,' Jacob growled.

'Both? No, I wouldn't do that.'

Jacob studied him. 'What's that supposed to mean?'

'You never think about suicide, Jacob? Never?' He shot a quick look Jacob's way. 'No, my guess is you don't. You're not the type.'

'You are?'

He shrugged. 'I change so fast I doubt that anybody, including me, knows what type I really am.'

By now it was close to midnight and traffic was on the negligible side. A few minutes later Buddy's building was in sight.

'Give her a message for me,' Kaganovich said as he pulled up in front of it. 'Tell her if she wants her letters—' He broke off and shook his head. 'Forget it. If she wants them she can damn well come and get them. What the hell is she afraid of?'

'You've got letters that belong to Buddy?' Jacob asked carefully. 'Is that what I'm supposed to understand?'

Kaganovich said nothing.

'If you do . . .'

'If I do it's between us,' he snapped. For just an instant he looked like a cossack eager to ride someone down. In the next instant he had changed again. His grin was merely taunting. 'Besides, you're not her keeper, Jacob. You just got through telling me. Maybe you're as self-confused as I am.'

Jacob got out of the car and started up the steps. He heard Kaganovich pounding after him.

'Wait, wait. Listen, Jacob, come on up to the Dunsany with me. There's this all-night blitz session going on. For pretty heavy dough. Tsarkov'll be there, which means I'll bust his ass for a lot. Which means he'll go damn near crazy. It'll be fun, I swear.' He took Jacob's sleeve, tugging persuasively—no warrior now but a small boy with a reluctant parent.

Jacob pulled free.

'Don't be sore at me,' Kaganovich pleaded. 'Forget I even mentioned the letters. They're nothing anyway. Hey, I'd never do anything to hurt Buddy. Let's go, OK?'

'Don't you ever sleep?'

'Me? No.' The grin again. 'You think if I could sleep I'd be playing all-night blitz chess?'

'I'll pass,' Jacob said. 'So should you. You've got a tournament on tap for tomorrow.'

'Yeah?'

'Don't you?'

'Maybe yes, maybe not. Maybe neither of us do. Hell, Jacob, we could be stuck in a time-warp.'

But Jacob continued up the stairs and this time was not followed. As he pushed through the front door on his way to the security check, he heard the roar of the motor. He stopped to watch Kaganovich catapult the Jag into a heedless reverse and a hurtling, screeching U-turn.

CHAPTER 6

You entered through a side door designated Dunsany Convention Centre, and there you found everything you needed to stage a major league chess tournament. Off to the right, ten yards or so, was the amphitheatre-like Canterbury Room. Ordinarily a ballroom, it was furnished with two

hundred cafeteria-style tables, butted up against each other
to form 20 long rows divided into three sections. The tables
were covered with clean white cloths and sturdy paper chess
'boards', each numbered to separate it from its brothers,
and later in the afternoon players from all over the country—
a smattering from all over the world—would be using these
as killing fields. They would be the lesser players, however.
The 40 'Open' players, including the tournament's half-
dozen authentic stars, would contend in one of the smaller,
flanking rooms, either the Cheshire or the Keswick. Con-
tinuing beyond the Keswick, you counted off three more
even smaller rooms: the 'Chess Store', where you could buy
all manner of equipment (scorepads, clocks, chess sets of
course, and a wide variety of books, ranging from self-help
to elaborate, full-colour chess histories. Also chess calendars,
posters of Bobby Fischer, and bumper stickers, proclaiming
that you made chess not war, or that your idea of heaven
was a passed pawn); 'Postings', where you went to learn
who your next opponent would be as well as to *post* the
result if you won (losers considerately absolved from that
responsibility); and 'Skittles', which was the lounge. There,
not surprisingly, you could play Skittles (another name for
blitz or speed or action chess), or eat your lunch, flirt with
a groupie, re-play your last game (victors tended to do this
more readily than losers) or nap if you were impervious to
decibel levels that could rise dramatically.

Jacob arrived early. Even so, the corridors were already
full of ebb and flow as players and/or spectators wandered
nomadically from room to room or sprawled out on the
furniture lining the walls, or clustered in front of one of
the promotional displays. These sold posters, or books, or
computers, or chess sets, some so gorgeously carved that
only a clod would regard them as functional. Jacob poked
his head into Skittles. Games were already in progress
despite the hour—9.0 a.m.—and each had its small though
highly verbal gallery. He joined one of these, enjoying the
swashbuckling aura always in evidence when chess was

played that fast. Not truly chess, purists said. Jacob supposed not, but whatever it was it was certainly fun.

His own bracket was not scheduled to get under way until
2.0 p.m., but he was hoping to watch the great ones for a
bit. Among them, Tsarkov had been designated first board,
and Kaganovich seeded only fifth. Considering how inactive
Kaganovich had been over the past few years, fifth was
probably generous, Jacob thought. Seedings and first round
pairings for his own bracket had not been posted yet, and
he crossed to the tournament director's table to ask when
that might happen.

There was a line of a dozen or so preceding him. Directly
in front were two young men both in dirty T-shirts and torn
jeans. They were discussing the always interesting subject
of prize money.

'How much is the Upset Prize?' This was the shorter and
slightly dirtier of the two. He had the round face of a
cherub and the cynical eyes of someone far older than the
twenty-five which was probably his age.

His companion's most distinctive feature was a shaven
head. 'What Upset Prize?'

'Upset, upset. You beat the shit out of someone who's
supposed to beat the shit out of you, that's an upset. Gotta
be an Upset Prize.'

'Maybe there does, maybe there don't.'

'Gotta be. Because if I was to win it, they'd sure as shit
be upset.'

Jacob grinned.

The tournament director was a harried-looking J. F.
Carrington, according to the nameplate on his paper-
swamped desk. He was short and plump with careful clothes
that seemed somewhat out of place amid the general
raffishness. Something about Jacob's size and bulk made
him twittery.

'Check the postings,' he snapped when Jacob asked who
he was scheduled against and where that great event would
take place.

'They don't seem to be up yet.'

'They will be.'

'When?'

'When we get around to it.'

Jacob guessed he didn't really mean to be nasty, merely dismissive—the line *was* growing ever longer. Still, he found himself reacting adversely and was about to become rude when a heavy-set red-headed man in his early forties exploded into the room. His cheeks matched his hair, and his body language was fluent in its expression of rage. Behind him sauntered a very tall, thin satellite with an air of aristocratic elegance, who seemed distantly amused.

The first man released a stream of what was almost certainly invective, though since it was in Russian Jacob could not have sworn to that. In excellent English the satellite (fifties, high cheekbones, cold blue eyes, curled moustaches) translated.

'Comrade Tsarkov is complaining about the noise coming from the corridor. He says the Keswick room sounds like a boiler factory.'

Tournament Director Carrington was struck to the heart. 'That's not possible. I wadded paper in the door to prevent any such thing. I myself put the silver duct tape—'

Another blast of vituperative Russian.

'Comrade Tsarkov describes your tournament as distinctly second-class. As . . .' At a momentary loss for a phrase he turned for some reason to Jacob, who supplied: 'Mickey Mouse.'

'Ah yes. Mickey Mouse. Mickey Mouse indeed. Comrade Tsarkov demands your personal assurance that spectators will conduct themselves in a civilized manner. Failing that, you will have his resignation instanter.'

Comrade Tsarkov underscored this with a snarl. A final burst of Russian across the TD's bows, and he was gone.

'In Moscow, Comrade Tsarkov says, spectators know their place.'

And with a charming smile for Jacob, the tall thin man followed Tsarkov.

'In Moscow you either know your place, or they stand you up against a wall and shoot you,' Carrington said to Jacob as if they were now conspirators.

Jacob said, 'Just the tournament directors.'

Leaving him to stew in his overheated juices, Jacob followed the Russians into Keswick, bright with the glow of luminaries.

Upwards of a hundred people were in the room, Jacob estimated, all forty of the 'Open' players—most of them rated 2200 and above—the rest spectators. These were spread about in irregular clumps. As individual games lost lustre the clumps tended to dwindle and drift, reshaping themselves behind likelier boards. The boards were set up on eight long trestle-tables. Tsarkov's protests to the contrary—or because of them, Jacob supposed—the room was quiet. The predominant sound was the distinctive noise of chess's double-clocks being hit. Players did this after making a move, thus stopping their own and automatically starting their opponent's. Pausing at the threshold, Jacob was struck by how young these gifted players were, late twenties on average. A secret sigh, then, for lost youth and opportunity.

Of the moveable clumps the largest was at the first board, Tsarkov's. His opponent was a black teenager in a wheelchair—one of three such chairs in the room—whose forehead glistened with perspiration. In fact both seemed equally tense. Jacob had the feeling Tsarkov spent every waking hour in that state and was one of those who regarded any other response to life as not merely frivolous but incomprehensible. Standing behind him, arms negligently folded across his chest, Tsarkov's attenuated colleague was in notable contrast. His languid gaze wandered from Tsarkov's board to various other salients as if in quest of something to use against boredom. But when it settled on Jacob, though only for an instant, he suddenly realized how very alert that gaze was.

The room's other major clump, almost as large as Tsar-kov's, belonged to Kaganovich, who looked remarkably fresh for someone who might well have blitzed the night away. He was against a young giant wearing a Manhattan Chess Club T-shirt and a smile that oozed confidence. Kaganovich had glanced up as Jacob entered. Seconds later he moved a piece, hit his clock, and joined him at the door.

'King Kong doesn't know it yet,' he said, 'but he has four moves left. How are you, my friend?'

'OK. You look OK.'

'I won seventy fish last night. Mostly from Tsarkov, who broke a mirror with his chess clock. I told you you should have been there.'

As Jacob watched, Tsarkov's satellite deserted his post, gliding over to form a threesome. He was smiling. 'A patzer, Dimmie. In the old days you would have done him long ago.'

Kaganovich smiled, too. Both smiles were mirthless. 'The KGB has asked me to make it look good. You understand how that works, Valentin.'

'Me? I understand nothing.' He put a hand each on Jacob's elbow and Kaganovich's and moved them gently towards the door. 'Except Tsarkov's sensibilities.' Outside, studying Jacob, he said, 'You are an old friend of Dimmie's?'

Kaganovich made his face go gangsterish. 'Who wants to know?'

Ignoring him, the Russian introduced himself. 'Valentin Gregorin,' he said. 'At your command, sir.'

Jacob said his own name, and the two shook hands.

'Are you a chess player?' Gregorin asked.

'A great one,' Kaganovich said. 'You can tell Tsarkov for me that my friend Jacob Horowitz is a chess-playing mole, so great a player that the CIA has been ordered to keep him under wraps for fifteen years, a period just coming to an end now. And that we are arranging to have Jacob be a last-minute entry. Do you think Tsarkov will be amused when you tell him that?'

'Tsarkov is never amused. And I will certainly not tell him that,' Gregorin said.

'I'm a patzer,' Jacob said. 'Nothing at all for Comrade Tsarkov to worry about. That is unless he worries about the action in the Under 1400 class.'

Gregorin sighed. 'Tsarkov worries about everything.' He bowed and started back into Keswick, but with his hand on the door he stopped. 'If you *are* an old friend of his . . .'

'A new friend,' Kaganovich said. 'But clearly a better friend than many old friends I could mention.'

'Me, Dimmie?' Sharply. 'I never did you any harm you didn't force me to.'

Kaganovich smiled. 'Then perhaps you are not among the old friends I had in mind.'

Their glances held for another moment. And then Gregorin turned back to Jacob. 'If you can, help him to be careful,' he said. 'He has never understood that survival requires a certain commitment to the task.'

When he had closed the door behind him Kaganovich said, 'Once we were very close. He was my teacher and my mentor.'

'I gather you're not close now.'

Kaganovich studied Jacob, eyes glinting with something Jacob at first thought was malice and then graded down to mischief. 'Gregorin brought the word,' he said.

'What word?'

'The KGB's word. Very cloak and daggerish, it all was. A handsome gold cigarette case with my monogram on it. One opened the case and found a single cigarette. One unwrapped the paper of this cigarette and found a two-word message: "You lose." What do you think of that, Jacob?'

'I think you might be making it up.'

He doubled over in a silent belly-laugh. 'Only a little here and there,' he said. 'I have to go inside now and polish off

Mighty Joe Young. Rendezvous at the hotel check-in desk. Half past seven?'

'What for?'

'We'll dine together, and I'll unfold for you "The Life and Times of Dmitri Kaganovich". Can you resist that?'

'Yes.'

'And I'll provide a chess tip or two guaranteed to raise your rating 75 points. Jacob, please. I need a solid man to talk to. Solid men aren't easy to find.'

Jacob shrugged and said all right.

'On me,' Kaganovich said, beaming.

About to follow him into Keswick, Jacob decided instead to first check back into Postings. Carrington was gone, but now 'Under 1400' was on display at last. He saw a young woman studying the chart, staring at it with an odd kind of patient anger, as if the chart were in league with forces that had a history of conspiring against her.

'I can't make head nor tail of it,' she said when he was next to her.

She was a small-boned blonde in her early twenties with a rather plain face, much of it obscured. She wore extra large, extra dark sunglasses for that purpose. Her hair was in a bun pulled old-maidishly tight, but it had a nice honey colour. A glance at the chart, and Jacob could understand why she was having trouble. The names and numbers were tiny, a helter-skelter scrawl. The lines that should have separated them were not drawn with anything like the same purposefulness as those on behalf of the 'Open' chart. Instances of the tournament director showing his big-name bias, Jacob decided. Still, after a few minutes he was able to penetrate the various mysteries. He learned that he was slated against someone named Hatcher, who had a rating near the top of their category, and that Foxy Farrington's first opponent represented no apparent threat to him. He was then ready to offer help. He asked for her name.

'Elaine (brief hesitation) Rowell.'

Having broken the code, he had no difficulty locating her

on the chart. He identified her opponent and gave her her
board number. She noted both in a little book withdrawn
from her purse and thanked him.

'Good luck,' he said.

She blushed, murmured something he took to be recipro-
cal and left. He looked after her thoughtfully and was not
surprised to see her head towards Keswick. He then made
some notes in his own small book, located a men's room,
after which he too headed towards Keswick. He found her
standing at the door as if she thought an incantation was
required to get it open.

'He may be out of there by now,' Jacob said.

She was startled. 'Who?'

'Your husband. You're Elaine Rowell Kaganovich, aren't
you?'

She blushed even more deeply than before. 'You know
Dimmie?'

He nodded. 'Would you like me to reconnoitre?'

'No,' she said. 'I'm perfectly capable of—'

She didn't finish. She broke off and started briskly away,
but she didn't finish that either. She paused, turned, and
came back. 'Forgive me,' she said. 'I'm a very shy person,
you see. And sometimes when I'm being shy I also find
myself being rude. The thing is, I really would like to know
how he's doing, but I'd rather he didn't think I'm . . .' She
looked away from him.

Jacob opened the door, stuck his head in, and then
reported: 'No sign of him. He said he was close to winning.
My guess is if you went back to Postings, he'll probably
turn up there pretty soon.'

'Thank you. Thank you very much, Mr—'

'Jacob Horowitz.'

Once more the flame was in her cheeks, but her voice was
surprisingly even. 'Are you related to Buddy Horowitz?'

'Her out-of-town cousin. I'm staying with her.'

She thanked him again, started away again, stopped
again. 'May I buy you a cup of coffee, Mr Horowitz?'

'Only if you call me Jacob.'

'And everybody calls me Lanie.'

Her smile made her almost attractive, and she seemed a
shade more relaxed as they went together to find the Dunsany's coffee-shop. They had two cups each. Over the first
they exchanged basic chess information, learning that for
both this was the initial tournament. They agreed it was
exciting. Jacob said he didn't expect to do well and hoped
mainly to avoid making a fool of himself. She said something
astonishingly different.

'I've always been pretty good at games. Not that I have
much natural ability, but I do have a sort of terrier quality,
and I often beat people I shouldn't. Dimmie taught me, you
know. He's a marvellous teacher. He says I'll win our
bracket.'

'Does he?'

'Yes,' she said. 'I guess I shouldn't have told you that.
You'll think I'm boasting. I'm not, though. It's just
that . . .'

'What?'

Her cheeks were scarcely even pink. 'I feel comfortable
with you. You don't know what an extraordinary experience
that is for me. The result is I'm talking too much.'

He tried to reassure her and was successful, so much so
that over the second cup he found her reviewing the events
preceding Kaganovich's courtship. A stopper had been
pulled. Words gushed.

'My Uncle Derek is president of Moresby College, and
my father sent me there so I could be watched over. I'm an
only child, and Daddy has never really thought of me as
trustworthy. Not that I blame him, of course. When I was
sixteen I ran off with our gardener's son, and having that
marriage annulled was both costly and messy. He was not
a very nice boy, the gardener's son. And I was aware even
then he was marrying me for my money. You do know who
my father is, don't you?'

'Yes.'

'Which is of course what Dimmie did, too. Marry me for
my money, I mean. Why else would he? I'm not exactly a
fool, Jacob. I know what I look like and what I am, for that
matter. I also know how good-looking Dimmie is, how
charming, and how sexually compelling. Women throw
themselves at him. They always have.'

'So I hear.'

'Your cousin did.'

'Did she?'

'All women do. Something happens to them, and they
can't help themselves. I don't blame her, you know.'

At sea as to what comment this called for, Jacob was
silent. So was she, long enough for him to think they had
exhausted the subject, but then she said, 'Dimmie never
would have married her. Does she think he would have? If
she does, she's wrong. Only someone like me could get him,
I'm afraid. Someone with money. I'm sorry for her. I really
and truly am. Still, I have him now, and I intend to keep
him forever.'

Jacob tried to hide the scepticism this generated, but she
saw it and smiled.

'You don't think I've got what it takes, do you?'

'I'm not sure you're the issue.'

'What do you mean?'

'I was just wondering if anyone has.'

The smile hung on for a count of two, but its life was
gone. She had forgotten about it, and it lay there, crumpled,
like something discarded. 'I guess I couldn't stand that,'
she said after a long moment.

He kept silent.

'Not having him, I mean.' She looked at Jacob as if
he were a mirror reflecting herself in some altered and
diminished state. 'His being someone else's, I mean.' She
had begun to shiver and had to hug herself to make herself
stop.

Jacob found it easier to glance away.

'He told you about Daddy, didn't he?'

'A bit,' he said cautiously. 'I gather your father keeps asking him to leave.'

'Ask? Daddy doesn't ask, he commands. Daddy thinks because he's lord and master of the Portland, Oregon building trades, that makes him lord and master of the universe. And so Dimmie infuriates him. Dimmie won't tug his forelock the way everyone else does. For one thing, Dimmie knows he doesn't have to. He's got an ace up his sleeve.'

'You?'

'Yes, me. I told you—I won't give him up. I never fought my father for anything in my life, but I'll fight till I die on this. He believes that now. When he came storming into my room last night, demanding that I come home with him, he thought I'd let him bulldoze me the way I always have. But I didn't. And I won't ever, ever again. Daddy believes me. They both believe me.' She paused. 'I would like it if your cousin believed me, too.'

'Believed what exactly?'

She leaned forward. Her whole upper torso seemed suddenly charged with energy, but instead of answering directly she said, 'If you could only understand what it means to have never wanted anything. Never. Until the morning I somehow found myself in Dimmie's Russian Lit survey, I was walking dead. A zombie. I never thought about anything, dreamed about anything, cared about anything. I was like some twenty-year-old bear, hibernating her way through life. That day changed everything. I came awake. I *am* sorry about Buddy. I've understood from the very first that she's a remarkable person. But what I want her to believe—what she *must* believe—is that Dimmie's mine. He can't be anyone else's.'

He watched her go. Thick, muscular legs; short, determined strides. It struck him suddenly that there might be more of her father in her than she knew.

Jacob lunched at Barney's, at the bar. Business was brisk. Between restaurant and bar, Barney and his staff of three— a cook, two waitresses—were kept hopping.

He nibbled at a turkey sandwich morosely. He wasn't really hungry. It seemed to him he was flirting with a cold. Usually that was the only thing that affected his appetite. He thought it also might be affecting his world view. Something was. He ought to be thinking about chess, enjoying a little anticipatory excitement. Instead he was thinking about a Russo-American gigolo, his poor-little-rich-girl wife, her industrial giant daddy, and of course his own will-o'-the-wisp cousin. Where *was* Buddy? Not hide nor hair of her since her door had closed in his face the previous night.

Barney pushed a beer in front of him. Because he hadn't ordered it, h⸱ looked up askance.

'Might do you some good,' Barney said. 'What's wrong? Let me guess—you miss Helen.'

'Among other things.'

'Other things. OK, you found out who you're opening against, and it turned out to be Kaganovich after all.'

Jacob forced a smile.

'He was in here again,' Barney said. 'About an hour ago, looking for Buddy again. What do you suppose is going on?'

'Did you ask him?'

'I'm asking you.'

Jacob considered his options and then said, 'They met on vacation, did you know?'

'No.'

'I gather the earth moved.'

Barney made a small puffing noise as if he'd had his stomach prodded. 'So that's what it was,' he said at length. 'Should have guessed. Hell, I remember now thinking I'd never seen her on that kind of high, I mean when she came back from Aspen.' He paused. 'Seems like I have been around Buddy in love.'

They were both silent then, recalling their conversation of the day before.

'They kept in touch,' Jacob said, 'and I got the feeling she was planning a visit out west when the bomb exploded.

Which is to say a Dear Buddy letter. You knew nothing about this part?'

He shrugged. 'He double-crossed her?'

'Well, not really. Curious fellow, Dmitri Kaganovich. Thoroughly undependable, and yet I don't think it's in him to lie. He made a commitment, found he couldn't deliver on it, and as he says, chickened out. Of course the complicating factor is he's still slightly nutty about her. I mean, he ought to leave her alone but he won't. Or can't.'

Barney rubbed hard at his favourite bar stain. His face was unreadable, or should have been in its lack of expression. And yet Jacob read something there that took him aback, something guarded but something hurt.

'Barney . . .'

'Beat it, Jacob. I got paying customers to attend to.'

Jacob watched him move off down the counter, his still powerful frame in the gorilla-like crouch that had begun (he'd once confessed) as an act and remained now as an inextricable part of his persona. A dumb phrase popped into Jacob's mind: Buddy and the Beast. He got rid of it as fast as he could. Glancing at his watch, he saw that it was a quarter of one. Time to get cracking, he told himself sternly. He hitched up his pants and went off to war.

CHAPTER 7

It had been almost a year since Helen had seen her, and the image she retained was of a tall, slender girl with bright red hair and eyes so vividly blue as to be almost mesmeric, though there was nothing in the least sinister about them. She also recalled a kind of residual gawkiness. That was history. The length and leanness had not been lost but transformed, sufficiently rounded so that what she knew she was looking at was authentic beauty.

Deirdre saw her come into the restaurant and stood. Men

looked at her; women, too, though more analytically, of course. Deirdre seemed unaware of the stir she was causing. Or rather, Helen thought, she was aware, all right, but experience had honed her style. Even a year ago she'd have shown her jitters. Now, what you saw was the calm of the battle-hardened.

They kissed.

Helen sat and said, 'If Tina Farrar could catch your act.'

'She'd have a cat fit,' Deirdre said, sitting, too.

Five year earlier, Tina and Deirdre had been dedicated enemies at the Byrd School, the plush academy for unfinished girls that had provided the stage for a murderous drama.[1] It was a drama that had grown out of their bitter rivalry, and one in which Helen had played a critical if not the conclusive role. The results had been diverse. But one of the good ones had been the friendship between Deirdre and Helen. Often interrupted over the five-year period, it showed no signs of being abandoned. Both women were interested in it. But it was Deirdre, more than Helen, who kept it flourishing. By and large, she made the calls that brought them together—as she had this one.

'She wrote me, you know,' Deirdre said. 'Tina, I mean. Invited me to her wedding. Surprised?'

'Nope,' Helen said. 'Part of the tension between you had to do with how much she liked you. And how much she wanted you to like her. Only you never beleived that.'

'At the time I didn't believe anyone liked me.' She paused, then reached out to touch Helen's hand. 'Except maybe you.'

They ordered lunch. Then Helen said, 'OK, you didn't haul me down to talk Tina Farrar and other old times. And what the hell goes on here anyway—I mean, famous Chicago watering hole and all that, for someone who's supposed to be a kidnap victim?'

'Are you sore at me for that?'

---

[1] *Death of a Nymph*

'For what?'

She shrugged. 'I know you, Helen. You're thinking shenanigans. Spoiled brat throwing a tantrum because she can't have her way. Well, if you had *him* for a father—'

'I might consider myself lucky,' Helen said.

Deirdre flushed. After a moment she said. 'Yes. Of course.'

'Shenanigans,' Helen said. 'Damn right.'

Deirdre looked up and smiled.

'Well, that's what it is, my dear, though I can think of less polite terms. Stop horsing around and come home. Talk it out.'

'Talk it out! How can you talk it out with a man who leaves the room the minute you raise the subject? With *two* men who do, actually. Fielding's no better. Between them, they're about to drive me mad.'

'Has it occurred to you that maybe they're right?'

The blue eyes became warning signals in a way Helen remembered. A little daunting. A hint of the unpredictable and/or the unpardonable. A chair could get knocked over. A coffee cup might be elbowed to the floor and smashed on behalf of psychological advantage. Deirdre was never afraid to be outrageous. But Helen beamed up messages for her own eyes to reflect and kept them unwavering.

'Right about what?' Deirdre asked softly.

'Fielding Gow may not be—'

'Don't!'

'The right man for you for a variety of reasons,' Helen finished calmly.

After a long moment Deirdre grinned and drew back. Like lowered flags her lids came down to cover her eyes, and when she reopened them they were merely blue. 'Do *you* think that?' she asked. 'Truly, I mean?'

Helen shrugged.

'Please. Don't back off like that. I count on you of all people *not* to back off. You know me. I'm not sure anyone knows me better. And you know I'm not a fool.'

'A bit quirky, if you don't mind me saying so. But no, not a fool.'

'I've experimented with others every now and again. I honestly have. There've been times when I told myself Fielding really is too much bother. The trouble is damn it I'm only half alive without him. There was this lovely man in . . . well, what difference does it make where. The point is how very decent he was. And how sweet. And kind. And how detestable I was to him because he wasn't Fielding. And yes, my dear, I understand about the Montagues and the Capulets. And the Gows and the Adamses. And I tell you that all the ridiculous family feuds in the whole world are not going to keep me from having what I must have. Even Fielding can't do that, and God knows he's giving it a shot. You're looking at me with that hateful poker-face of yours, but I know damn well you know exactly what I mean. You know how I know?'

'How?'

'Because nothing and nobody could have stopped you from having Jacob. Even Jacob.'

Helen kept silent.

'Could he have?'

'No.'

'Did he try?'

'Well, there was that week when he kept insisting he wasn't good enough for me.'

They were both silent then as they concentrated on the pleasures of perfectly cooked soft-shelled crabs. Actually there was little need for further conversation. Both understood that the subject had been adequately covered and tacit agreement reached. Helen would do what she could.

But after a while she said, 'You really mustn't expect too much, though. The thing is, your father's one of the most rational men I know. And when rational men go berserk . . .'

Deirdre looked unhappy. 'I know, I know' she said.

Helen sighed. 'I just figured out why you kidnapped

yourself. Because you were pretty sure if you did your father would call me in.'

'That's pretty much your fault, too.'

'It is?'

Deirdre glared at her. 'Because I knew if *I* asked you to help, you'd tell me it was none of your business.'

CHAPTER 8

Perry Hatcher (United States Chess Federation rating: 1350) was a nice young man from Akron, Ohio, who queened a passed pawn after three hours of struggle. Defeated, Jacob felt unashamed, and they went together into Skittles to reconsider and replay. Five games to go, Jacob counted off. And to the ghost of his father pledged a victory.

To his surprise he found Buddy at home. She was on the phone when he entered and blew him a kiss. He stowed his chess stuff in his room and returned to the living-room. By then she was in the kitchen, fishing martinis out of the fridge. She handed him his. He sipped.

'OK?'

He smacked his lips.

'Well, how did you do?' she asked brightly.

He told her. Though far from a serious player, she did understand the rules and appeared to listen with interest and enthusiasm. But he knew it was a performance. He ended his report.

'And who do you play next?' she asked as brightly as before.

'Don't know yet. Won't until the schedule's posted tomorrow.' He paused. 'Kaganovich won both his games today. So did Tsarkov.'

She nodded.

After a moment Jacob said, 'I told him I'd have dinner with him tonight.'

She smiled, brightness intact. 'Good.'

'Do you mind?'

'No, no, no.'

'If you do mind—or if there's a chance we . . .'

She came to him, put a finger to his mouth and cut off the rest. 'I'm rotten company these days, Jacob, my pet, and I feel guilty about it. At least this way I'll know you're being entertained. Whatever else he is, Dmitri *is* entertaining, isn't he?'

'Yes.'

She looked at him. 'What else is he, Jacob? I mean aside from charmer and con-man? Is there anything else to him? Have you come to conclusions?'

'No.'

She nodded. 'And you're smart if you never do. Because surer than hell you'll conclude one thing and in that instant Kaganovich the chameleon will be another. For instance: I bet you think he's an honest scoundrel.'

He kept silent.

'And I bet you think he loves me.'

'My guess is—'

'Fool, Jacob. He's flimflammed you. He loves no one. Not even himself. That's right, Jacob. Dmitri Kaganovich doesn't even love Dimmie. So what chance did anyone else ever have?' She took a step back and clenched her fists. Her knees had flexed a bit, though Jacob doubted she was aware of this. She looked a little like a tailback waiting to go student body right. At the same time she looked fragile.

'Buddy . . .'

'What?'

He hesitated a moment, the moment it took to decide caution was a commodity that, if you didn't throw it to the winds, could wind up damn near choking you to death. 'Who are you sore at? Kaganovich, or someone else?'

'What someone else could that be?'

'In six months you would have eaten him alive. He knew

that. It's what made it absolutely necessary to run for cover.
You must have known it, too.'

'The someone else I'm sore at is me?'

He nodded.

'Why exactly?'

'One, because you think you behaved like a love-sick fool.
And two, because it never did take much to get you sore at
yourself.'

Instinctively, then, he reached out for her in case the
words stung more than he intended, but the tailback spun
away from the linebacker and left him with air in his grasp.
Once more her door slammed shut, forming two countries.

Jacob sighed. He went to the window and stood there,
staring out at the boats in the harbour. There were a lot of
them. As he watched, it seemed to him they had begun to
arrange themselves in formation so they could spell out
messages: big-mouth, buttinsky, idiot . . .

CHAPTER 9

'All unhappy families are uniformly boring,' Kaganovich
had said at the outset of dinner, 'and there ought to be a
law against talking about them.'

After which he had plunged with gusto into the story of
his. It had been of course vastly entertaining—picaresque
in quality, ironic in tone, and though certainly not ham-
strung by truth there was some of that in it, too, Jacob felt.
Politically radical parents with a tiny American viper in
their bosom. Flesh of their flesh, though everything about
him—tastes, opinions, attitudes, predilections, even his as-
tounding chess talent—was incomprehensible to them. Hos-
tilities on a daily basis in that household. When they took
him off to Russia it was, in effect, as a prisoner of war. But
through chess he had earned a parole. Marked for special
attention, he was also removed somewhat from his parents'

control. Tournaments all over the country. Publicity. Favour. Nothing but good things at first, including the mentor-like friendship with Valentin Gregorin, and the amusing enmity of Boris Tsarkov.

'God, how he hates me,' he had said with intense satisfaction.

And now, in one of the Dunsany's lounges, Kaganovich vs Tsarkov was on yet again—blitz chess. About twenty spectators had gathered to witness. Twenty plus, Jacob noted. He had spotted Lanie lurking in the doorway. He nodded at her encouragingly. She smiled and came further into the room but behind Kaganovich, concealed from him by a small forest of bodies.

Tsarkov was trying mightily to look relaxed.

Kaganovich *was* relaxed, joking with the crowd.

Five dollars a game.

Five minutes on the clock for each player. Victory to come either as the result of checkmate, or to the one who did not use up his time.

In blitz chess the brain sizzles, but it's not really thought being generated. Instinct is closer. Hands move quickly. Chessmen are captured at an alarming rate. Positions are of course fluid and their intrinsic value always enigmatic.

The two played as their natures compelled them to— Kaganovich imperturbably, shifting pieces smoothly and hitting his clock with minimum display. Tsarkov's clock showed its bruises, the result of constant pummeling by a heavy, remorseless fist.

As the game approached its climax the spectators became jittery—whispers, murmurs, shallower breathing, shifting feet. All were as intent as the players themselves. Not Jacob, nor anyone saw the big, beefy man enter the room— arguably the first time in his mature life an entrance of his had caused so little stir.

But in the next second all became aware of him. He kicked over the chess table. Pieces went flying. Tsarkov screamed his outrage.

Had he been minded to scream, Kaganovich could not have because the intruder's hands were on his throat. It was then Jacob had his first glimmering as to the intruder's identity. When he saw the horror in Lanie's face he knew he was right. He started forward. All things considered, his reaction time had been excellent. Even so he was too late.

Valentin Gregorin was not a young man—or one who looked particularly strong—but it became instantly apparent that you'd like him guarding your back. Jacob never saw precisely what he did. It all happened too fast for that. But by the time Jacob reached the struggling pair they were no longer struggling. Kaganovich was free and gasping for air. The intruder was against the room's far wall, bent double, moaning, and comforting savaged privates.

Lanie's comfort was for Kaganovich, not her father.

Gregorin made eye contact with Tsarkov and started for the door. Tsarkov looked sulky and rebellious but the speed with which he caved in gave Jacob fresh perspective on their relationship.

He beat them to the door.

'KGB training?' he asked Gregorin.

Quizzical eyebrows in innocent v's.

Jacob elaborated. 'Whatever it was you did back there, it was pretty slick.'

'Are you arresting me for it?'

'No.'

Smiling. 'One hardly needs KGB training for basic judo.'

Tsarkov muttered something interrogatory.

'Nyet,' Gregorin said. 'Enough chess for one day.' And to Jacob: 'When that man recovers his wits he will probably wish to launch an international incident. Please, for both our sakes—for our country's sakes—make it difficult for him. Who is he, by the way? Do you know?'

'Dimmie's father-in-law,' Tsarkov said in only slightly accented English. 'And he might have killed the son of a bitch if you hadn't interfered.' He made a sullen, heavy-footed exit. Gregorin grinned, then followed.

Tsarkov's English was controlled by switches, Jacob decided. Off when the need was to be tactically mute. On, maybe, for your basic death threat. He turned back to the tableau in the room.

By now Royal Rowell had been helped to a sofa by several of the spectators. Kaganovich and Lanie had disappeared somewhere. Jacob toyed with the idea of doing likewise, but Rowell saw him before he could bring that off.

'You there,' he said. 'I want a word with you.'

He was Jacob's age and as large as Jacob, possessing all the vestiges of a former offensive tackle or guard: thick neck, meaty shoulders and bay window gut. Hair losing to bald. Eyes small and red-rimmed. Mouth self-indulgent. Jacob didn't feel much like talking to him but found himself waiting for Rowell to join him.

'Are you the Russian fairy's friend?'

'Which Russian fairy is that?' Jacob asked politely.

'Start with the one who blindsided me, the one I saw you talking to just now. I'll get to the other in a minute.'

'No,' Jacob said.

'But you know who he is.'

All in all, Jacob felt justified in repeating the negative.

Rowell gave him his best boardroom glare, clearly expecting a withering. 'You're lying to me,' he said.

Jacob kept silent.

'Are you a goddam Russki, too?'

Jacob identified himself.

Rowell was enraged. 'A cop, and you let him get away with that shit? A goddam cop, and you let an unprovoked attack on a respectable American citizen happen right under your nose without doing a thing to stop it?'

Jacob looked at his watch. 'Big day tomorrow,' he said and took a step towards the door.

Rowell stopped him. 'Now wait just a damn minute,' he said.

Jacob stared at the bear's paw grasping his arm until Rowell knew he had a decision to make. For just an instant,

Jacob saw, Rowell thought of getting back a bit of his own, but some insight connected to his survival mechanism persuaded him to back off. He released Jacob's arm.

When free Jacob said, 'I met Dmitri Kaganovich yesterday for the first time. I have absolutely no influence over him, if that's what you're getting around to. And now good night.'

Once more Rowell stopped him. This time with the changed quality of his voice. 'A friend of his would warn him never to underestimate me,' he said. Quieter, he seemed, paradoxically, more dangerous. And the words, Jacob thought, constituted good advice.

When he unlocked the door of Buddy's apartment the phone was ringing. He was short by a step and a half, but picked it up anyway.'

'Hello!'

Getting no answer, he slammed it down and in the same vexed tone shouted for Buddy. No answer to that either.

He went in to the bedroom to get Helen's phone number, and while he was searching for it in his notebook, the phone rang again. He grabbed it hurriedly.

'Jacob . . .?'

Vexation vanished. 'Was that you a moment ago?'

'No,' Helen said. 'Just now got in. How are you?'

Health and welfare bulletins were exchanged. Then they brought each other up to speed on the status of their respective family dramas. The daughter in hers, Helen said, was now reunited with the father, more or less.

'What's more or less?'

'She's back under his roof, but promising further incidents of an unspecified nature unless certain concessions are made.'

'What concessions?'

'That's for the go-between to find out. I'm the go-between. Might just add a day or so, Jacob. I'm not saying it will but it might.'

'And if I said no?'

Just a heartbeat of extra silence at the other end. The tone that followed was neutral, delicately balanced, conveying not much more than a reasonable interest in the question raised.

'*Are* you saying no?'

'No.'

'Oh my God, I didn't even ask how your game went.'

He told her. They then arranged to be in contact the following night and hung up. Jacob felt unsettled. Revisionist thoughts danced in his head, and he stared at the phone ambivalently, wanting to pick it up, wanting it to ring again. And suddenly it did. This time, however, Kaganovich was on the other end. He sounded as if he might have been drinking.

'I've been trying to get you for hours. First, you're not there, then your line is busy. You're ducking Dimmie?'

'Perish the thought.'

'Did you see what that devil tried to do to me? He tried to kill me. Want to hear why?'

'Don't I already know?'

A giggle, then the superseding burble of liquid being imbibed. 'Not the latest, Jacob. There's been a development, a further indignity heaped on that Royal pain in the ass. Listen. He came to my room this afternoon. Proposition: seventy-five big ones if I could make Lanie hate me enough to turn loose.'

'Big ones. Would that be hundreds or thousands?'

'Thousands, thousands, man. We're talking Royal Rowell here, not some jumped up parvenu. We're talking giants of industry. *Now* what do you think of your Dimmie? You impressed?'

Jacob acknowledged that he was.

'And listen to how smart the son of a bitch is. Not just to blow town. No way. I have to make her hate me, or else we both know she'd mount safaris.'

'I'm waiting for the indignity. You're telling me you turned him down?'

'What I told him was I'd have to think about it. Later I sent him a note. It was the note that got to him, I guess.'

'What did you say in the note?'

Giggle, plus slurp. 'Hundred and fifty or no deal.'

'And that got to him? Little thing like that? You ought to thank your lucky stars for Gregorin.'

'A shrug. How do you make a shrug over the telephone?'

'Why a shrug?'

'The KGB giveth, and the KGB taketh away.'

'He really is?'

'Since the day he was born.'

Jacob thought about that and what it might mean and came up empty. Then he thought about Royal Rowell enraged and wished there was an inhibiting piece of wisdom he could pass on to the man who had so heedlessly brought about that state—but knew there wasn't. So he said, 'Has it occurred to you that when Rowell shows your note to his daughter that might make her sore, too? I mean sore enough to save Daddy a bunch of those big ones?'

There was a moment of silence. In a voice that seemed to reflect a recovered state of sobriety, Kaganovich said, 'I hope it does.'

'Why?'

'For her sake.' Pause. 'And maybe even a little bit for mine. But you know what?'

'What?'

'It won't. Good night, Jacob. Hey, wait, wait. Hold on there. Almost forgot the real reason I called. Know why I called? Wanted you to be the first to know. You listening?'

'I'm listening.'

'Your Dimmie's going to win this goddam Capa. I really am. Didn't think so when I decided to enter. That was just craziness, to bug Tsarkov. But I think so now. I'm seeing combinations like I never did before. It's wild, Jacob. It's like poetry. God, I wish I could say that to Buddy. In Aspen when we . . . Jacob, I could say such things to her. I mean I could find *words* for things, such wonderful things. That's when you know it's special, right?'

'Yes,' Jacob said.

'You're my solid man, Jacob. I knew you'd know.' Pause. 'I'm going to win this Capa and dedicate it to her. You tell her that, Jacob. Tell her nothing can stop me.'

Part Three

END GAME

In the ending, the king is unexcelled as a means of causing damage.

I. Chernev

CHAPTER 1

Foxy Farrington had won his first game, Jacob learned in Postings Sunday morning. So had Lanie won hers. And it was she who was scheduled to be Jacob's next opponent: Canterbury in an hour.

As he noted this information he heard someone behind him mutter, 'Children should be seen, etcetera.'

He turned to see a small spidery man of indeterminate but great age. His face was criss-crossed with deep lines, and only a few strands of the much photographed Einstein-like mop remained. His blue eyes, however, could still glint impishly. Jacob knew him at once: Isaac Ackerman, several times American champion and his father's chess idol.

'Were you speaking to me?' Jacob asked, a real possibility since they had the room to themselves.

'No,' Ackerman said. 'I was speaking to myself. And the Deity. Did you hear the words?'

'Yes,' Jacob said and repeated them.

'Do I have your sympathy?'

Jacob checked the chart and saw that Ackerman was to meet the brilliant American teenager, Dahlgren, rated sixty points above him. Ackerman smiled.

'But last night I saw him consume a huge box of buttered popcorn plus three giant chocolate bars. I bought the last two myself. So maybe today biliousness. Maybe even appendicitis. Do you know what Ruy Lopez said in his little sixteenth-century book of advice and counsel?'

'No,' Jacob said, though Kaganovich had told him.

Ackerman told him again.

Yielding to impulse, Jacob said, 'My father belonged to the Manhattan Chess Club, and he was one of twelve boards against you the first time you appeared there.'

'What is his name?'

'Horowitz. He's dead now.'

'I remember him well. A beautiful player.'

Much of Jacob recognized this instantly as a charming lie, but that was the hip or civilized part. The primitive in him seized passionately on what he wished to be true, and he felt for a moment tremendously uplifted. But then as he watched the bent old man inch towards one of those little deaths, joy was transmuted, chilled by the immutable logic of the life-cycle. Jacob sucked in his gut. Hell with it, he told himself. Warriors ain't thinkers and thinkers ain't warriors, deciding that wasn't the worst locker-room counsel he'd ever had dropped on him.

He found Lanie already in her assigned place, a book open on her lap, the dark glasses firmly in place. She looked as if she'd been planted there.

'I knew it would be you today,' she said when he joined her.

'How?'

'I just knew. Just like I almost always know anything that's going to happen to me before it does. Anything important.'

'How's your father?'

'He left a note under my door last night asking me to call but I didn't. I couldn't. And I couldn't this morning.' She paused. 'I don't know how Dimmie is either. I wanted to be with him last night, but he wouldn't let me. He said he was in a dark Russian mood and needed to be alone. So I spent the night in my own dull company.'

'You're not dull.'

'Please don't be nice to me. It feels so patronizing.'

'I'll tell you the truth, Mrs Kaganovich. You're too flaky to be dull.'

She stared at him.' Really?'

'A kook from Dubuque.'

Her very good smile appeared, grew, and seemed as if it might have a lasting effect when suddenly it was gone, replaced by her game face. This was acceptably tight-lipped, narrow-eyed, and, in general, competitively contorted. 'I'm going to beat you,' she said. 'You know that, don't you?'

'Nope.'

'Well, I am.'

'I guess we'll just have to wait and see.'

Her hand shot out. 'Good luck, anyway.'

Almost at once he discovered he was the better of the two. She was too cautious, so much a by-the-book player that she missed opportunities. By the time they reached the twentieth move he felt he had achieved a distinct positional advantage. Soon thereafter he snatched a pawn and later another, so that in the end game he found himself with two passed pawns and no realistic way to lose. Her game face was history, having been replaced by expressions that ranged from dour to glum to grim. It was then the chess dybbuk took a hand. Jacob allowed a check he could have prevented, not seeing—until too late—that it was a *perpetual* check, that nothing he could do would release him from it as long as she wanted him there. Thus, his glorious passed pawns were doomed to advance no further: stalemate, a draw.

She looked at him. He acknowledged his plight with a rueful nod, and she brightened at once. She got up, stepped swiftly into the aisle. Suddenly she broke into a wild, though silent war dance—noiseless leaps, soundless whoops. He watched in astonishment. No such war dance had seemed possible to her.

'A draw, a draw. Oh, my goodness, how did I ever get a draw out of a mess like that? Come,' she said, seizing his hand to drag him after her. (One of the assistant tournament directors was bearing down on her to restore decorum.)

'Where?'

'To Skittles, of course. We have to replay the game move by move so you can learn where you went wrong.'

He followed her far from eagerly, yet with a flagellant's sense of the fitness of things.

They never reached Skittles. They passed Postings on the way and found it in uproar. Carrington, the tournament director, was on the phone. A crowd of a dozen or so was gathered around him, buzzing excitedly. In a voice that grew progressively louder until it ended in a shrill scream they heard him say, 'Yes, yes, *yes!* Are you listening to me, Stephen? If you have to break down the goddam door, break it down. I'll take the responsibility.'

Jacob saw Gregorin at the fringe of the crowd and joined him. 'What's going on?'

Gregorin's glance flicked to Lanie. 'Do you know where your husband is, Mrs Kaganovich?'

She shook her head. No animation in her face now, only the pale set of foreboding. 'Is that whose door . . .?'

Gregorin nodded.

Carrington slammed down the phone. 'Stephen will get back to me in ten minutes,' he said, speaking at large. 'If he doesn't, I'm calling the police.'

No foreboding there that Jacob could see. Instead the smug self-satisfaction of one who had shown he was capable of command.

Lanie touched Jacob's shoulder. 'Why the police?' Her voice shook a little. 'Dimmie got drunk last night and overslept, big deal. Why call the police for that? He'll be furious at all the fuss, won't he be?'

'Yes,' Jacob said.

'He really will be terribly, terribly angry.'

'Where's Tsarkov?' Jacob asked Gregorin.

'Back in his room, pacing,' Gregorin said. 'They awarded him the victory two hours ago, but he still thinks it's some kind of Dimmie trick. Only he can't figure out what.'

Jacob looked at his watch. It was almost half past four. 'Has he ever done anything like this before?'

'Once or twice. Usually when there's a—' He broke off.

'He means when there's a woman involved,' Lanie said.

Gregorin smiled apologetically.

'Of course. That's exactly what it is,' Lanie said. 'My heavens, all this fuss. And I'd be willing to bet anything he's with your cousin.'

Relief showed in her face but so did the effort required to get it there.

Jacob went to Carrington's desk and asked if he could use the phone. The man in absolute control of things was about to refuse, so Jacob flashed his badge. Carrington did not examine it closely enough to rob it of authority. He made room and Jacob came around to the far side, back to the crowd.

When he dialled Buddy's direct line office number he got no answer. He dialled's Barney's.

'Haven't seen her since yesterday,' Barney said.

'Do you expect her?'

'Nope. Hey, Jacob, it's a zoo in here today. Busy as hell. If she turns up or calls I'll tell her you're looking for her.' He hung up.

'Busy as hell' at half-past four? Why? A sudden city-wide notion that the hop crop was suffering irreversible blight? He shrugged. Turning, he saw that Lanie and Gregorin were both gone. And that Carrington had been joined by a beautifully tanned young man in a maroon blazer with a gold-threaded Dunsany logo over his breast. His nameplate identified him as Stephen.

'Tell him,' Carrington said, nudging him in Jacob's direction.

The young man wet his lips but kept silent.

'Do it, Stephen, it's purgative. Don't I always know what's best for you?'

Stephen sighed. 'Actually, Arnold and I and the police found him about an hour and a half ago,' he said. He paused. 'Does he know Arnold?'

'Never mind about Arnold,' Carrington said firmly. 'Go on.'

'They wanted it kept quiet. The police, I mean. Oh God, it was so . . .'

The young man tightened his jaw, his fists, his diaphragm, and then broke for the rest-room.

'Purgative,' Carrington said with satisfaction. 'He'll feel better now.'

Jacob took off for the Dunsany lobby.

When he entered he saw Gene D'Agostino at the front desk talking to a clerk who looked familiar. That was because he looked like Stephen, though the nametag on *his* maroon blazer proclaimed him Arnold. Having been waved over by D'Agostino, Jacob arrived in time to catch the tail-end of what Arnold was saying.

'And that's the last I saw of him.' His voice was agitated enough to suggest he might be prepping for a run similar to Stephen's.

D'Agostino was gentle. 'Take it easy, son. What time was that, can you tell me?'

'About six-thirty. Stephen and I were working late shift because Felix Esterveldt had one of his heads. Anyway, that's when it was because I said to Stephen—'

'Did you notice anything unusual about him?'

'Unusual?'

'Well, had he been drinking, for instance?'

'Oh yes. But with Mr Kaganovich that wasn't unusual.' Arnold smiled brilliantly, and for a moment or so seemed restored to health. But then up came his hands to cover his eyes. 'Oh my God, I can still . . . I don't think I'll ever forget it. Not as long as I live.'

D'Agostino patted his shoulder. 'Arnold has been out-standing. It was Arnold who found a master key when no one else could and unlocked the door for us.'

'Ugly, ugly blood,' Arnold said, shuddering.

A guest wanted her messages and Arnold, still shudder-ing, went to get them for her. D'Agostino moved Jacob a few feet down the counter, far enough to be out of earshot.

'Gays and chessies, hotel's full of 'em,' he said sourly. He looked at Jacob. 'Probably they're the same thing.'

'What ugly blood?'

D'Agostino raised an eyebrow. 'Thought you knew.'

'Kaganovich? He's dead, then?'

'Dead as a bullet from a Colt thirty-five automatic can make him. He ain't in his room any more, but I can take you up there if you want.' He paused and then *carefully* casual, Jacob thought, added, 'That is, if you got any interest.'

Jacob nodded. It was a nod he managed with difficulty; his head seemed too heavy for easy swivelling. Nervously, reflexively, he reached around to rub the back of his neck, and it was like stroking ice. *Had* he known? Of course he had, but a fierce effort to resist the knowledge had somehow been mandatory. Now for a moment awareness over-whelmed him.

But D'Agostino didn't notice. He appeared to be undergoing his own inner turmoil. Eyes hooded, hands deep in his pockets, he rocked back and forth, accompanying this with tuneless whistling. Finally he found words. 'Thing is this is likely to be an extravaganza before it's through. News-papers, television, the whole media ball of wax. No, the guy wasn't a movie star, still . . .'

'Self-inflicted?'

'What?'

'The wound. Did he shoot himself?'

'Damn it, Jacob, slow your motor. I got something to say to you first, OK?'

'OK.'

'The nub of the situation is, there's this boss I don't like and who sure as hell don't like me. It'd be Christmas in July for him if I was to screw up. And I'll tell you, it could happen. I'm not that smart. I mean, I'm better than average as an administrator. And terrific as an office politician. But smart like you I never pretended to be.'

Jacob made an impatient gesture.

'All right, all right, I'm almost there. I don't *want* to screw up, Jacob, not one little bit. The way I figure I might avoid doing that is with your help.'

'My help—how?'

'You're booked into town till the end of the tournament. That's two more days. I'll take the two for starters. Who knows, maybe you'll work a miracle. After that . . . hell, maybe I'll have a conversation with *your* boss. You see where I'm headed?'

'Dimly.'

'But you're probably standing there, thinking—what's in it for me? One, I don't mind you taking a bit of credit. Two—hey, Jacob, I could be commissioner here some day. Since when does it hurt for a *mahoff* to owe you a favour?'

Jacob was silent.

'Besides,' D'Agostino said with a shrewd look, 'I just got a flash. I don't have to sell you on this much, do I?'

'Why don't we go on up?' Jacob said.

In the elevator D'Agostino told him the ME had tentatively put time of death between ten and eleven p.m. 'Not carved in stone until after autopsy. You like the way ME's always say that? Who's asking them to carve anything in goddam stone? Could even go as late as midnight he says, like he's doing me some kind of favour by even opening his little black bag.'

'Kaganovich was alive after eleven,' Jacob said.

'How do you know?'

'He phoned me.'

D'Agostino looked at him. 'What'd he say?'

Deleting Buddy from the conversation—on the grounds that D'Agostino had not yet established a need to know—Jacob confined himself to Rowell's offer. He then reported the blitz game and the attack by Rowell that had interrupted it. 'It was about half past nine when that all got sorted out.'

'And that's the last you saw of him? Kaganovich, I mean.'

Jacob nodded.

D'Agostino was whistling tunelessly again. 'I hate it when guys with power and influence turn out to have motives,' he said.

They were in the corridor now, a few doors short of

Kaganovich's room. Jacob stopped abruptly. 'I don't,' he said.

Friendly jab on the upper arm. 'Just a joke, Jacob, for God's sake. You don't know Serpico when you see him?'

He got Jacob back in motion.

Twenty-one twelve was a suite for the rich and famous. Thick, earth-coloured pile rugs, an amphitheatre of a bathroom, a walk-in fireplace, a handsome walnut bookcase—short on books, long on entertainment centre—a lavish display of museum-quality prints, and furniture polished and brocaded enough to salve a materialist's fiercest itch. How Kaganovich must have relished it all, Jacob thought, experiencing in the next moment an empathic pang and then a metaphysical shiver at how easily the mind adjusted its tenses.

But D'Agostino seemed impervious to intimations of mortality. 'We've been through his stuff,' he said. 'Not that he brought all that much.' His glare seared the room as if indicting it and its contents for not being more forthcoming. And then for an instant softened appreciatively: 'Still, what there is is choice.'

He moved about, opening drawers and allowing Jacob to browse among socks, underwear, and monogrammed shirts. In the closet hung an expensive navy blue blazer and white tropical trousers. Gleaming black grosgrain loafers and white calfskin dress shoes were aligned beneath them. As D'Agostino had suggested Kaganovich had been travelling light but stylishly. No insights to be derived, except the rather surprising one that he'd been basically neat.

'He burned some stuff,' D'Agostino said when they came up to the fireplace. 'Papers, looks like. Burned hell out of whatever it was. All he left was an ash or two. Lab boys took that.'

Papers? Buddy's letters? Perhaps a suicide note—of which nothing as yet had been said? An extra death threat or so? And of course half a dozen other possibilities equally as likely. Jacob confined himself to a nod.

At length they arrived at the desk.

'The big finish,' D'Agostino said, eyeing it antagonist-ically. It was as if the desk only seemed inanimate, was in fact capable of coming to life at any instant, whereupon a back room and a rubber truncheon might do it some good. 'Untouched, except for the departed, who departed for the morgue about fifteen minutes ago. I'll show you photos as soon as I get a set.' He kicked the wooden foot harder than he'd intended. Wincing, he said, 'Hope this son of a bitch enlightens you more than it did me.'

Jacob could tell he meant that deeply, and suddenly he had a hunch. It was when D'Agostino went one on one against the desk and lost, Jacob guessed, that the idea of out of town help began taking shape.

But at first glance the desk didn't spill its guts to him either. A computer chessboard held the centre, its scaled-down pieces flanking both sides. Not much else marred the shiny walnut surface. A well-ordered, unremarkable, perfectly ordinary desk, except of course for the triangle of dried blood at the right front corner. Stemming from this was a narrow double path—not unlike a particularly long cowboy's string tie—that worked its crooked way to about the middle of the leg.

'It *wasn't* self-inflicted,' D'Agostino said suddenly.

'How do you know?'

'No note. And I've seen enough suicides in my time to lay money on the pattern. No note, and none of the other earmarks either."

'What are the other earmarks?'

'You telling me you think it was suicide?'

'At this point I'm not telling you anything,' Jacob said. 'I'm asking.'

A few more bars of tuneless whistling. "OK, I just put together a hypothetical. It's nine forty-five, you with me? Kaganovich is up in his room now after the fracas in the lounge. He's restless, but he sets up the chessboard and works at it, studying, because he's got a tough game the next day. That's what chess champs do, don't they?'

'Who enlightened you?'

'Every chessie I talked to. That's right, isn't it?'

Jacob agreed it probably was.

'And he did have a tough game coming up—with Comrade Tsarkov, right?'

'Yes.'

'OK, but like I say, he's restless. Too restless for real good concentration, so he calls you. You're not there. Back to the board, but off and on he keeps trying to get you on the phone. Finally he does. You talk. What time would you say you finished? Eleven-fifteen thereabouts?'

'Thereabouts.'

'Back he goes to the chessboard. But now he's got no stomach for it at all—your conversation didn't help much —so he puts the pieces away and just as he's finished there's a knock at the door. No sign of forcible entry, so whoever's there is known to him. He lets him in. Or her. Or *her*. Could just as easily have been a bimbo, given that tomcat's reputation. I know what you're thinking. No sign of forcible entry, but no sign of another presence either. OK, that's what makes this only hypothetical, right?'

'Go on.'

'Dialogue between the two. Don't ask me about what because I don't know. But it heats up. Gets so goddam hot Kaganovich goes for his gun. Struggle. Gun goes off. Kaganovich is hit, perp lugs him to the desk. Why not? What's to lose? Maybe we'll think it's suicide even without a note.' D'Agostino looked pleased with himself and rather surprised, as if he'd done a better job than he'd expected to. 'Any major holes? Major ones now, not itty-bitty ones.'

'Do we have the gun?' Jacob asked.

'Sure. Didn't I tell you? It was in his hand. Colt thirty-five."

'You said *his* gun. Do we know that?'

'We're checking. But it figures to be, don't it? Hell, what

kind of a goofball murderer leaves his own gun behind and expects us to believe suicide? Think about that.'

Jacob started to reach for the chess board, stopped himself, and looked at D'Agostino questioningly.

'It's been dusted,' D'Agostino said. 'Everything has, but I can tell you now what the fingerprint geniuses are eventually going to get around to telling me. The only good prints are Kaganovich's.'

Jacob overturned the board but could find no pieces left in the carrying pocket. He had begun to puzzle over this when he heard D'Agostino mutter something in self-deprecation. He looked up to see him pointing. Jacob followed the direction indicated and found, at the base of the far wall, another dark stain. This one much smaller, half-dollar sized.

'Sorry. Forgot to mention that,' D'Agostino said. 'It's where he took the bullet.'

That helped a bit with the puzzle, Jacob thought. He glanced back at the desk, then at the stain he was standing over, then at the bed the stain was close to, and finally at the phone *that* was close to. 'I don't think he was dragged to the desk,' he said. 'I think he got there by himself.'

'How come?'

Jacob's "hypothetical' clarified. 'What it must have been is he knew he didn't have enough left in him to complete a phone call. I mean, he knew he wouldn't be able to punch out 911, for instance, wait for an answer, and then manage to put something into words. So he got himself to the desk instead.'

'To do what?'

'Leave a message.'

'What the hell are you talking about?'

Jacob brooded for a moment and then said, 'Did you take a good look at the body?'

'I goddam memorized it.'

'OK, be Kaganovich for me.'

D'Agostino shrugged, but then unhesitatingly sat down

at the desk. He found a position for his head a precise inch off centre, eyes left. His upper chest was pressed against the desk's front edge but carefully skewed to the right so that blood from a gushing wound would flow inevitably in that direction. His right hand was fisted around an imaginary revolver. His left hand hung down.

'Just about like that,' he said crisply. 'OK?'

'Tell me about the left hand.'

'What about it?'

'Yours is dangling between your knees. Was his?'

For the first time D'Agostino seemed uncertain. 'Damned if I know,' he said finally, a confession. Then, ruefully: 'Hell, I just flat out didn't notice. None of us did.'

'All right, you can come alive again,' Jacob said.

D'Agostino revitalized himself. 'So what kind of message?' he asked.

'The kings are missing,' Jacob said.

D'Agostino looked blank.

'The chess set's kings. They're not on the desk and not in the carrying pocket. My guess is if you call your ME you'll find they were somewhere on Kaganovich, maybe in his fist, the dangling one.'

D'Agostino hurried to the phone. While he was there Jacob recalled Kaganovich on being beaten and paraphrased him for D'Agostino's benefit when he returned.

'He really hated it,' Jacob said. 'Made him physically ill, *that* kind of intense. All right, even a dying man is gripped by the habits of a lifetime. He already had the bullet in his chest. There wasn't anything he could do about that. But sending the message . . . it was reflexive, the irresistible drive to stay in the game.'

D'Agostino stared at him. 'Jacob, you are one brilliant son of a bitch,' he said almost prayerfully.

'The ME found the kings?'

'Wrapped in the left fist, the goddam dangler. My face is red.'

Jacob started for the door.

D'Agostino beat him there, barring it. 'So he left us a message. But what is it? What am I supposed to do, send out an APB for a king? This is America, greatest country in the world. There are no kings.'

'I'll be in touch.'

'Yeah, all right, but there's something I want to know now.'

'What?'

Though D'Agostino rubbed chin and mouth vigorously this produced nothing in the way of articulation. Jacob understood then it wasn't knowledge he sought so much as company. He just wasn't quite ready to be alone.

'Tell me about him, Kaganovich,' he said finally.

'Tell you what?'

'I don't know, something. OK, tell me about him and your cousin. Foxy Farrington says Kaganovich was carrying a torch. Was he?'

'If Farrington already told you, why ask me?'

'All right, don't get sore. I take Foxy with the same grain of salt you do. And I know about his own torch, OK?'

Jacob nodded.

D'Agostino buried his hands in his pockets and, head down, walked a tight cabalistic kind of circle. 'Damn, I wish I could see where this was all going. And damn, I'd like to believe I'll still be on track at the end of it.'

Jacob started for the door again, but again D'Agostino got there first. 'Just tell me, was he likeable?'

'Yes.'

D'Agostino suddenly saw this in a blazing light. 'Maybe too likeable?'

D'Agostino, Jacob thought, was the quintessential hip-shooter. Hip-shooters traded accuracy for speed, of course, but it didn't follow that they *always* missed. Jacob waited with interest to see where he would come out.

'I mean, he was so goddam New York smooth, for a Russki. And don't tell me he wasn't a Russki. He was. No matter what you or his pal Barney Hogan have to say about it.'

'All right, a smooth Russki. So what?'

'So maybe a Russki spy?'

Jacob was startled.

'You think that's loony tune?'

Well, maybe not so loony tune after all, Jacob decided. What did *he* know about the KGB, except it probably moved in mysterious ways. So he told D'Agostino what he felt might be true about Valentin Gregorin and watched the other fasten on it with growing excitement. Before Jacob was quite finished he was back grabbing for the phone. 'We got him. We got our man. My whole gut's vibrating.' By this time he was punching out numbers. Moments later he had uniforms under way to Gregorin's room. He put down the phone, grinning, spirits dramatically on the rise. Clearly he now felt in his element, taking action, giving orders.

'What charge?' Jacob asked.

'You his lawyer? Who said anything about a charge? An invite to parley a bit, that's all. Hey, maybe I want the other one along, slap him in the next cell.'

Jacob refused to be helpful. 'What other one?'

'You know damn well what other one. Kaganovich's arch rival. What's his name. I said it a minute ago.'

'He's KGB, too?'

D'Agostino considered the possibility and then said, 'As far as I'm concerned, all Russkis are KGB unless proved otherwise.'

'Hey, hey, American way,' Jacob said.

'All right, only some Russkis. Suspicious-looking ones with good covers who could be spying their brains out while us poor damn Yanks think the only things they give a damn about are gambits, or whatever the hell they're called.'

'His name's Tsarkov,' Jacob said, while deciding firmly *against* telling D'Agostino about the death threats. He'd save them for a less fervid time.

At the phone once more D'Agostino was widening his

invitation list. Then he said, 'To you this spy business in bullshit, right?'

Jacob shrugged.

'Your view is Kaganovich was just another Brooklyn boy, not a hell of a lot different than you or me. OK, but just for argument's sake, suppose the Kremlin don't see it that way. Maybe they see him as a traitor, a dirty no-goodnik defector. What do they do? They call in the KGB and say off him. How far-fetched is that?'

'Or maybe Kaganovich was KGB and whoever offed him is CIA.'

D'Agostino looked dismayed. 'Jesus, is that a joke?'

'More or less,' Jacob said.

The phone rang, and as D'Agostino went to pick it up, the glance he shot at Jacob contained very little amusement. 'Yeah?' And a few minutes later: 'All right, put a couple of blues where they can watch the door. Call me back the minute anything develops.' He hung up. 'Not on the premises,' he said. 'Neither of them.'

'Have they checked out?'

'No.'

Jacob made his third foray for the door.

'Where?'

'I'll be—'

'Yeah, yeah, but *where* are you going?'

'Someplace quiet to do some thinking.' He paused. 'About motives closer to home.'

'Like what, for instance.'

'Like an enraged father, for instance. Or an unhappy wife.' He said nothing about a woman scorned and waited a second to see if D'Agostino might. He didn't. When Jacob left he was staring daggers at the silent phone, as if it, too, were the Kremlin's thing.

CHAPTER 2

On reaching the lobby Jacob went at once to the front desk. This time it was Stephen on duty, buzzing busily back and forth among the Dunsany's trade. Busy ignoring Jacob, too. It was as if he construed him somehow as a figment from a guilty past. Jacob sighed, recognizing the syndrome. Cops are nightmare figures. Even in the blameless they stir mysterious fears of Kafka-like punishment. He watched for a while and then made throat-clearing noises as a prelude to flashing his badge. He hoped it had retained talismanic powers. It had. It got him the number of Royal Rowell's habitat, which turned out to be on the same side of the building as Kaganovich's but a floor below. He knocked. The door was opened almost at once.

Superficially at least, this was a different Rowell from last night's poltergeist. This one smiled when he saw Jacob.

'Come in, come in, been expecting you,' he said. He motioned towards a chair in a suite that, colour-scheme aside, twinned the one Jacob had just departed. Blues and greens replaced earth tones—appropriately enough, Jacob decided. There was something *anti*-earth tone about Rowell. Despite the bluff, peppery, quick-fisted exterior he liked to present, Jacob thought he was ice-cold at the core. Something decadent about him, as if only a civilization in its declining stages could have produced his particular kind of corruption.

'Done a little checking on you,' he said. 'And I now know who you are.'

'Who am I?'

'Dick Tracy,' Rowell said, expanding a display of remarkably strong white teeth. Jacob wondered if Rowell enjoyed his resemblance to a barracuda and decided he did.

'Drink?'

Jacob declined.

There was a tall pitcher of colourless liquid on a table at the right of the sofa. Jacob supposed it was gin, and from it and the bottle of bitters adjacent Rowell built himself something that pleased him. He sipped appreciatively.

'Sure?'

Jacob shook his head.

Rowell took another sip, then stretched out on the sofa, cradling his drink on his chest. He seemed very comfortable and relaxed, not at all like a man whose motives for murder were as discussable as in fact his were. He wore a faded blue sweatshirt with a *Fortune* Magazine logo under a legend proclaiming money as the great equalizer. Chinos. Scuffed loafers over sockless feet. Nothing about him suggested the least eagerness to be part of some other scene. Jacob was disappointed.

'Do you know where my daughter is?' Rowell asked but without urgency.

'No,' Jacob said. And then added, 'The last time I saw her she still thought her husband was alive.'

Rowell sipped.

'Did you kill him, Mr Rowell?'

Another carnivorous flash. 'Negative. Or had him killed either, though the thought crossed my mind once or twice. And I know lads who would have done it for me.'

'Is that so?'

'Damn right it's so. Portland is a city packed full of them.'

This was another syndrome Jacob recognized. Everybody wants to impress a cop. It made him tired, and he rose to go.

'Hey, I've got an iron-clad alibi. Don't you want to hear it?'

'Tell it to Lieutenant D'Agostino.'

Rowell swung himself to a sitting position. 'Hang on a minute there, Tracy. I've got something to tell *you*. Something you'll find interesting. Who knows, maybe even useful.'

Jacob waited.

Rowell took another sip, regarded his glass as if what he saw reflected there constituted a body of persuasive evidence and then said, 'You don't like me much, do you?'

'Almost none, actually,' Jacob said.

It chopped a bit of the smile away at each corner, compressing the rest into undiluted menace. 'You're a friggin' wise guy, ain't you, Dick? Back in *my* bailiwick I know how to deal with wise guys. I'd take you out on the boonies somewhere and personally beat the shit out of you. And if for some reason I couldn't do that I'd find some other way to break you. And it would give me pleasure, a whole lot of it.'

Jacob kept silent.

'As far as Kaganovich is concerned, that's one cheap, conniving, fortune-hunter less in the world. Someone did me a favour is the way I look at it. If I knew who I'd repay it. Which is why I'm talking to you now.'

Jacob raised an eyebrow.

'Somebody saw someone you know here last night,' Rowell said. 'And told me because I paid for the information. I'm passing it on to you, gratis. To you, you understand? Not to—what's-his-name?—D'Agostino.'

'That's it?'

'That's it,' Rowell said. 'Favour repaid. And now get the hell out of here, you wise-assed son of a bitch.'

Jacob rose, lifted the pitcher from the table and emptied the contents over Rowell's head. Rowell spluttered, swore, got to his feet, and was shoved back down hard enough to almost topple the sofa. Unhurriedly, Jacob walked to the door.

Rowell was no longer cool.

'Don't come to Oregon,' he screamed. 'Come anywhere near it, and by God I'll show you what trouble is.'

'It'd almost be worth the trip,' Jacob said without turning.

CHAPTER 3

He found Buddy at home. She seemed calmer, more self-possessed than at any time since his arrival in Philadelphia. This was something of a surprise to him since within very few moments of his having opened the door he had learned from her that she knew of Kaganovich's death. In jeans, white sweater, and no make-up, she sat on her sofa sipping Scotch and water. She looked a shade tired, but not as if she were in any way bereaved. He sat in a club chair opposite her, feet up, sipping his own Scotch and water—drink and hassock provided by her—and then because he thought she wanted him to, he queried her about her lack of emotion.

She shrugged. 'He was a worthless man over whom I once made a fool of myself, to use your phrase. Not the only such case in my chequered history. I'm sorry he's dead of course, but the fact is I've been recovered from Dimmie for quite some time—though you don't believe that.'

'How can I?'

'Why not? Oh, I know what you want to say—that I've been . . . out of sorts, not myself, the past few days. That was Dimmie's fault. I don't mean because I still had any real feeling for him but because he was creating all this turmoil around me. All this craziness, the incessant phone calls, turning up here, there, and everywhere, attempting to get me to . . . God knows what. The badgering, the bedeviling . . . Jacob, no wonder I was upset. And then of course the suicide threats.'

He studied her.

'You didn't know about the suicide threats?' she asked.

'No.'

'On the hour, every hour. Damn it, don't look at me like that.'

'Like what?'

'As if I were Lady goddam Dracula.'

Peering into his glass, he saw there a wreath of coal-black mums inscribed: 'From Lady Dracula'. It made him wince.

'Jacob, you are such an outrageous sentimentalist. That big body and street-smart mug of yours hides it, but it's true just the same. Does Helen know that about you?'

He said nothing.

She slammed her glass down on the table hard enough to shake up a pair of pre-Columbian fertility dolls that had been placidly camping there for years, sending them into a frantic survival dance. 'Who did *he* ever grieve for, the late Dmitri Kaganovich? No one, of course. You have to care in order to grieve. He *was* worthless, Jacob, and knew it better than anybody. Worthless but no hypocrite. And I don't think you should be one either.'

'What does that mean?'

'It means finish your tournament and go on home to your Helen.'

'I see. Who told you he was dead?' Jacob asked.

'Foxy Farrington, who else? He loved telling me. He stuck his head in my door and said, "Kaganovich got wasted." Just like that, the first words he's spoken to me in seven months. And then while he furnished details he *watched* me. God, how I hate that man. Anyway it's in the afternoon edition and all over the air waves. Not just the locals, the networks, too. Dimmie would have adored the attention.' She aimed a hand at the TV set. 'Do you want me to turn it on?'

He shook his head. 'Where were you last night?'

Her chin rose pugnaciously. 'Ah, I do believe we're getting to it.'

'What?'

'The grilling. Should I send out for the stark white light now or wait until you really hit stride?'

He stared at her. 'What I'm trying to do is help. I'm

trying to get the truth from you. These days that doesn't seem as easy as it once was.'

'Help? Help what?'

He kept silent.

'God almighty, Jacob,' she said, eyes shut, fingers pressed hard against her temples, 'you are such a bore. All right already. From eleven to half past twelve I was in Barney's. As a matter of fact, I was there hoping you might drop in.'

'Were you with anyone?'

'I was alone.'

'But Barney saw you, of course.'

'Of course.'

'And he'll swear to it, of course.'

'Why on earth wouldn't he?' She regarded him unblinkingly until the phone rang. She picked it up and a moment later said, 'It's for you. Gene D'Agostino. You'll want to take it in your bedroom, of course.'

He wanted to whack her. 'Of course,' he said.

When he picked up the bedroom phone he heard the other click off at once, ostentatiously.

'Anything?' D'Agostino said.

'Anything what?'

'You know . . . *kings*.'

'No. I haven't had—' But at that moment something did pop into his mind, blocking what he was about to say.

D'Agostino urged him on. '*Tell* me.'

'Rowell's first name,' he said. 'Royal.'

'Yeah? What about it?'

'Kings are royal. I mean—what the hell, Kaganovich didn't have all the time in the whole world.'

'You serious?'

'I'm not sure . . . Yeah, I think I am.'

'But why two kings?'

That, Jacob thought, was needlessly quick of D'Agostino. 'I don't know. Maybe it doesn't matter. Maybe . . . it does,' he finished lamely.

D'Agostino was supportive. 'Hey, take it easy. You're

doing great. All that's wanted is for you to think on it some more. In the meantime I guess I got something for you. He just called—Rowell, I mean. He and his daughter are leaving town. Should I stop them?'

The thought of Rowell—eyes rolling, teeth gnashing— stomping around some local slammer in a choking rage was pleasant to him. But then good sense took the fun out of it. 'No. If we need him we can always find him.'

'Jacob . . .'

'What?'

'He told me something else. Something maybe you're not going to like too much.'

Jacob waited, certain he could guess what was on the way. He was right.

'He said someone saw a young woman in the Dunsany lobby about ten-thirty last night, a woman connected to Kaganovich.'

'Who's the someone?'

'He wouldn't say.'

'Go on.'

'She was recognized, Jacob. It was Buddy.'

'How was she recognized?'

'Come on. Buddy Horowitz ain't exactly Jane Doe in this town.'

'All right, let's say this someone's imagination is not working overtime. There could be half a dozen reasons for a journalist to be in the Dunsany lobby. And what do you mean—connected? Connected how?'

'She was seen there the day before, *with* Kaganovich. They were on their way to the Dunsany Grill, presumably for lunch.'

After a moment Jacob said, 'Ten-thirty is a bit short of what you need, isn't it?'

'Yeah.'

'And the lobby is twenty-one floors under Kaganovich's suite.'

'Right.'

'Still, maybe you ought to re-think your choice of rabbi.'

'Speak to you later,' D'Agostino said and hung up quickly, nipping debate in the bud.

Jacob took a bit longer. He stared at the phone unseeingly, seeing Buddy instead. Buddy, all her life an almost compulsive truth-teller, lying blatantly now. Why? What was she frightened of? As he restored the phone to its cradle, he realized how unsure he was that he wanted to find out.

The doorbell rang. He heard Buddy in response, heard her being answered—though that was muffled—heard her steps en route to the door, heard the door being opened, heard her gasp. He reached the living-room at the double, then stopped abruptly when he saw who was there: Lanie, .22 in hand, aimed menacingly—if not too steadily—at Buddy's head.

'Stay where you are, Jacob,' she said without turning towards him, voice as tremulous as her fist. 'I haven't yet decided what I'm going to do. Don't push me to anything.'

By now Buddy had recovered enough equilibrium to be breathing normally. She had even managed a slight smile.

Lanie looked at her. 'Did you kill him?'

Buddy shook her head.

'I don't believe you. Look, you're not even nervous. My hands are trembling. Yours are perfectly steady. You *could* kill a man if you wanted to. Couldn't she, Jacob?'

'Put down the damn gun,' he said.

'No.'

'Put it down before you blow your foot off. Then we can talk.'

'About what?'

'About whatever the hell you want. It's your agenda. Buddy, go get her a drink. Get her some Scotch.'

Buddy turned instantly, heading for the kitchen.

'Come back here at once,' Lanie shouted after her. 'At once, or I'll shoot. Don't think I won't.'

Buddy didn't break stride. Lanie started to cry helplessly,

huge pear-like tears forming instantly and rolling down her cheeks.

Jacob took the gun away from her and conducted her to the sofa where he sat next to her, stroking her shoulders until they settled to neutral. When that happened Buddy handed her her drink.

Lanie took a deep breath, then a deep pull on the whisky. She stared at Buddy. 'Did you love him?' she asked this time.

'Once.'

'And then you stopped? How do you stop a thing like that?'

'You make yourself.'

'I don't see how that's possible.'

'It's possible. All you have to be willing to do is bust your hump. I was. When I fell in love with him I thought he was a god. When I found out he was a shit I had a question to answer. Was I the sort of person who could be in love with a shit like that? I decided I wasn't.' She bent forward and cupped Lanie's chin, raising her face so she could study it. 'You aren't either.'

Lanie drew back sharply. 'You're wrong,' she said. 'I love him. I'll love him always. It doesn't matter that he's dead. I'll never stop loving him.'

Jacob, lifting his drink and staring into it, said, 'He wasn't a shit.'

Buddy looked at him. 'What was he, Jacob?'

'Something better than that,' he said. 'And he deserves to be mourned.'

Now their glances held. Hers was curtained, revealing only the vague outlines of things being hidden, like sheeted furniture in a shut down house. She got to her feet wearily and began a curious sort of wavering retreat, moving away from them as if on one wing. But at the door of her bedroom she stopped. 'If you want to help someone, Jacob, help her. You can't help me.'

Lanie watched in fascination. When Buddy had locked

herself away she shuddered, as if on beholding imprison-
ment forever. 'But she still loves him,' she said. 'As bitterly
as I do, doesn't she?'

Jacob kept silent.

Suddenly composed, she stood up. 'I made a fool of myself
as usual, Jacob. Thank God you were here.'

He held the tiny pistol out to her. 'You wouldn't have
used it,' he said.

'Wouldn't I?' She smiled. It took effort, but it was a real
smile none the less. 'Not even to blow my foot off?'

He reached for her purse and buried the .22 there. 'Where
did you get it, incidentally?'

'A birthday present from my father when I was eighteen.
He gave it to me so I could protect my virtue.'

'Does he own one?'

'Of course. Couldn't you guess that about him? A much
bigger one.'

'How big?'

Her hand flew to her mouth. 'Oh my God, that's not an
idle question, is it? You think—'

'Where was he last night, say between eleven and twelve?
Do you know?'

'Jacob, the point about Daddy is he's a bully. He only
beats up on those who are scared of him, like me. Not
Dimmie. Dimmie wasn't scared of him at all. It was the
other way around.'

'He didn't seem particularly scared of Dimmie when he
tried to break his neck earlier in the evening.'

'That was different.'

'How?'

'It just was. He lost his temper, don't you see? That's
not the same as going up to Dimmie's room to commit
cold-blooded murder.'

'My guess is there wasn't anything cold-blooded about
that murder. Whoever did it didn't plan to do it. My guess
is it happened as the result of something else that happened,
once he or she was in the room.'

'What?'

He studied her hard but then shrugged. 'I don't know,' he acknowledged.

She was silent a moment. Then, her smile luminous, she said, 'Anyway, none of that matters. Daddy couldn't have been in two places at once, and the fact is he was with me.'

He recalled that Dimmie had once placed her in a category headed by Joan of Arc. He thought her face reflected that kind of ennoblement now. He also thought she might be lying, but he wouldn't have wanted to bet on that either. Clearly, she was hypertense, but then she almost always was.

'With you where?' he asked.

'We were strolling. Back and forth, circling the hotel more or less. He was trying to talk me into going home with him.'

He kept studying her.

'It's the truth, Jacob.'

He put his arm about Royal Rowell's iron-clad alibi and walked her to the door.

'Promise you will, Jacob,' she said.

'What?'

'Mourn for him. He liked you so much.'

'Wouldn't it be more to the point if I promise to find his killer?'

'No.'

'No?'

She shrugged. 'I don't much care about that. You do, and my guess is you won't rest until you get it done. But it won't bring him back, will it?'

She kissed his cheek. Then something odd, something ambiguous came into her eyes. Pressed to interpret, he would have said part impulse, part challenge, and part ancient female cussedness. And then he would have added that it need not have been any of the above. But when she kissed him this time it was open-mouthed. An instant later she was gone, leaving him staring after her.

Buddy paroled herself. 'Will she be all right?' she asked.

'Why didn't you hang around and find out?'

She smiled. 'I could tell she didn't want me to. It was you she wanted comfort from, not me. And I don't blame her.'

He studied her morosely, not knowing what to make of her either.

CHAPTER 4

That evening Jacob won his first game. In slightly over two hours he beat an undersized, truculent, banty rooster of a man, veteran of sixteen tournaments, who until then had not been defeated in this one—a heady feeling. Anthony Peruzzi was not a graceful loser. He accused Jacob of sandbagging. Familiar enough with the term to know it was derogatory, Jacob suspected it might have an extended application here that he was missing. He asked for clarification. Peruzzi grudgingly supplied it.

'A sandbagger is a rat,' he said particularizing Jacob with a glare. 'Like he's unrated, see. And what he does, he plays in a New York tournament, for instance, beats a lot of guys who weren't prepared for him, then gets himself the hell on the Jersey Turnpike to a Pennsy tournament. Before the USCF, which don't move too fast anyway, gets a chance to upgrade him, he gets to do the same thing all over again— play in a lower bracket than he belongs in. Which means he bushwhacks some honest Joe like me and gets a terrific shot at prize money.'

Jacob, pointing out that his three-game total was a not very prizeworthy one win, was less persuasive than he might have hoped.

'Rats always got something up their sleeve,' Peruzzi said.

And skulked off towards Skittles.

Jacob, happiness unimpaired, hurried to Posting to proclaim his first victory.

'Miracle in Philadelphia. Jacob Horowitz found some cretin he could beat.'

Jacob brought the record up to date before turning to confront Foxy Farrington.

'He had a heart attack right after castling? A stroke? You paid him two hundred bucks? What? You can tell me. I'll swear a blood oath to secrecy.'

Nodding politely, Jacob crossed the room to the bulletin board. There was to be a gathering on behalf of Kaganovich, he'd learned from one of the assistant tournament directors. Carrington would officiate and friends would be invited to speak. Jacob wanted to check on time and place. Ten p.m. in Skittles. Jacob made note of the information.

'As ye sow,' Farrington said from under Jacob's right ear.

Not for the first time, Jacob yearned for an *Alice in Wonderland* type pill, a supplement of some kind that could be sneaked into Farrington's food chain, adding enough pounds and inches to his frame so that a self-respecting man could knock it about without having to hate himself for it afterwards. But pills such as that being in short supply, he knew his only recourse was discipline.

'Are you following me for any special reason?' he asked mildly.

'Don't be absurd. I have better things to do with my time. It's a free country, isn't it? I go where I want to go, even to that thing.'

'What thing?'

He motioned disparagingly to the bulletin board. 'Kaganovich's wake. And listen to everybody wax mawkish about a Russian ass-hole.'

'Kaganovich was on your hate list, too?'

'I liked him less than I do you, if that can be imagined.'

'How come?' Jacob asked, though he was certain he knew.

'Put that question to Jezebel, your whorish cousin.'

Despite himself, Jacob took a step towards Farrington who adeptly skittered out of reach. Ten feet away, he remained poised to skitter some more, peering at Jacob as if he wore a red coat and carried a hunting horn. But seeing that Jacob was again under control, he inched back. 'She killed him, you know. Which is what he had coming to him, true enough, but she'll pay for it. How will it feel to be related to someone on Death Row?'

He departed, but for some seconds thereafter a foxy grin seemed to hover in the air.

Jacob took deep breaths until the granny knots in his stomach loosened to simple slips. He was about to turn away when another bulletin board exhibit caught his eye. It had been half obscured by the message morass that surrounded it: tournament announcements; requests for rides to various salients around the country; offers of chess equipment for sale; offers of lessons; an offer of a photographic series titled *Bobby Fischer in Exile*, and the like. The exhibit in question was one of three biblical quotations. Two were handwritten and similar to each other also in their warnings of Armageddon. The third, however, was neatly typed on an unlined three by five card:

> And the carcase of Jezebel shall be as dung upon the face of the field . . .
>
> *Kings II*

Jezebel struck him, but not quite as forcefully as *Kings II*. He took the card into custody.

It was past midnight when the phone rang, waking him. Waiting for Helen's call he had fallen asleep on the sofa.

'So you're still alive,' he said when he knew who it was.

'Sorry, Jacob. I knew you'd be worried, and I wanted to call earlier, but it was impossible to get to a phone. All hell broke loose tonight.'

She sounded bone weary. He knew that but decided to pretend to himself he didn't. He growled something unsympathetic, wishing at the same time that he could shove a sock in his mouth.

'Don't you want to hear?' she asked.

'I want to hear how and when my wife and I will be living under the same roof the way married people are supposed to. That's what I want to hear.'

Pause. Tone a shade cooler. Not icy yet, but showing clear-cut potential. 'Well, Jacob, you can hop a plane in the morning and be here in jig-time.'

He upgraded his growl to a mutter. Her response: an extended silence. He knew that the Apache in her had now been released. If he could see her cheekbones they would look higher. Her eyes would be darker and more remote, and she would be wearing stillness like a serape. As always, this unnerved him. He didn't exactly apologize, but he did sort of grunt his way through an act of contrition, which she—veteran married person—chose to regard as acceptable.

She then told him about George Adams's atypical burst of violence that had resulted in a bloody nose for Fielding Gow, followed by ten minutes of non-stop hysterics from Deirdre. Doors slamming all over the place.

'I was like a whirling dervish, Jacob. First, I had to argue Fielding into staying in the house long enough for me to stanch the blood. Next, I had to dash upstairs and persuade Deirdre to unpack the bag she already had half-packed, preparing to leave forever. She didn't really want to, of course. Leave, that is. The fact is she thoroughly adores her father. Anyway, by the time I got back down George himself had gone storming off into the night, as had Fielding. So I've spent the last couple of hours unsuccessfully combing the neighbourhood for either one of them. Wherever he is, I hope George has recovered some. I've never seen him like that—George Adams, the quintessential "I'm in control" man. But right now everything's quiet. Fielding called a little while ago, and whatever he said pacified Deirdre, at least temporarily. She's asleep. And I keep hoping the next sound I hear will be the return of the prodigal father. Jacob, you think I should call the cops?'

'Where's the hotshot Adams hired as security guard?'

'Night off. I'll give George an hour. You think?'

'Yeah. What caused the blow?'

'Damned if I know, really. I doubt George himself could tell you. But to me it also looks like the quiet man syndrome. Which is what, you ask? Well, a quiet man goes along, goes along, reaches a limit—and then sometimes he just ker-booms! You know how that can be, Jacob.'

'I do?'

'No one knows better.'

A grunt, a mutter, and other similar forms of non-verbal communication.

'Jacob?'

'What?'

'Do you love me?'

'Uh-huh.'

'Say it.'

'I said it yesterday.'

'I'm on a quota?'

'Maybe I'll say it tomorrow.'

'Maybe I won't want to hear it tomorrow.'

Yeah, he said to himself darkly. That possibility, unexorcizeable, stayed burr-like in his brain, despite his absolute conviction that her feeling for him was deep and abiding. These conflicting ideas made him nervous, goading him, every so often, to test her—a form of behaviour that in more rational moments he could only regard as deplorable. But now the words tumbled out: 'I love you, I love you.'

'Good. Tell me about your games. You won one today, I'll bet.'

'How do you know?'

'That's what you're so sore about, mostly. You won, and I wasn't there to hear it all.'

So he told her. And then about everything else that had happened, realizing as he did how remarkably eventful the day had been. After hearing of the death of Kaganovich she was silent a long moment. Then she said, 'Apaches have a phrase. Translated it means, "Man with doom in him". I never met Dmitri Kaganovich, but is it outlandish to apply that to him?'

'No.'

'*Was* he suicidal?'

'Maybe. I can't make myself believe that's how he died, though.'

'All right, but is it in your mind that whoever killed him did him a favour?'

He considered that. He had done so before during the course of the day; now he did it definitively. 'No,' he said. 'My guess is he had no interest in dying just yet.'

'But you make him sound such an unhappy man.'

'Yeah. Still, in an odd kind of way I think he was used to that. I mean, it didn't seem to lessen the pleasure he took in certain things. That Jag of his, for instance. And of course he was so tremendously competitive. Didn't seem much like a potential suicide, the man who told me how absolutely convinced he was he'd win the tournament.'

'Maybe Tsarkov was equally convinced?'

'Convinced which way?'

'Kaganovich's.'

'And so?'

'I'm thinking about your kings,' she said slowly, carefully, as if land-mines were in the area. 'What I'm thinking is a tsar is a kind of king, right? Tsar, Tsarkov.'

He swore softly. Kings now everywhere you looked. *Royal* Rowell, *Tsar*kov, and let's hear it for the Old Testament. Enough kings now for a king-sized civil war.

'Jacob . . .'

'What?'

'I'm going to say good night.'

'Adams is back?'

'Good night and sweet dreams.' She hung up.

Jacob held the phone, staring at it. For just a moment he did consider calling the airport for flight information. Then he put the phone down and found his empty bed. For a while he tried to think productively. About kings and related things. He couldn't, and soon the phrase 'cabbages and kings' became a refrain that set his teeth on edge. So he thought about Kaganovich's Wake instead. He thought about what had been said there. And what hadn't been. More than a hundred had crowded into Skittles in response to Carrington's call. A dozen or so had risen to speak, all well-meaning. They had liked him, some quite a lot. Among them a few had been moved to tears; one black-clad young woman—whom no one seemed to know—to hysterics. But none, Jacob thought, could make you feel they had a key to him, clues to his mystery. What kind of man was he? Several had tried to answer, but the words seemed hollow. Pertinent to some feeling of loss perhaps, but not to the oddball Kaganovich. Gregorin hadn't been there, nor Tsarkov. Nor had Buddy or Lanie been there to . . . what? God alone knew. Truthful women who lie put heedless forces into motion, forces of an incalculable nature, that much he was sure of, though not much beyond that.

Truthful women who lie. Did that describe them? Both of them? If so, when and when not? If each had spoken of her dead lover would it have sounded remotely like the same dead lover? Would their speaking of him have made a difference? A sudden, machine-gun-like burst of sneezes sat him up. Not *yet* a thing of history, this benighted summer cold. Tissues. Aspirin for the headache that had delivered a pre-emptive strike at his left temple. Back to bed where the man with doom in him was lying doggo. Kaganovich, he felt, was of the breed who takes enigma to the burial ground. Unknowable but not unlovable. Let *that* be his epitaph, Jacob decided. He said goodbye to him and amazed himself by falling asleep.

CHAPTER 5

At the two-hour mark sixteen-year-old T. J. Moberly from Eleuria, Kentucky, asked Jacob for a draw. It had been one of those sticky, positional games that inevitably mutes the joy of battle. Yawning, the boy said, 'I'm bored out of my skull.' Jacob acknowledged that he was, too. Together, then, they went to Postings and updated their records. On parting, they shook hands warmly, each pleased to have settled the matter and be out of the other's sight.

Gregorin tapped Jacob's shoulder. 'That lad's sister and father are also entered in this tournament. All three have ratings low enough for dogs to urinate on them. None has won a game, and yet all seem to be having a good time. Not very American of them, is it?'

Jacob stared at him.

Gregorin stared back. 'You construe that as an unfriendly remark?'

'Yeah.'

'Forgive me, but I am feeling unfriendly today. You see, one of your compatriots murdered a remarkable compatriot of mine.'

'Is that a fact? Funny, but I've been thinking along the same lines. Only different.'

'How different?'

'Namely that he was iced by a KGB hit man, namely you.'

Not the twitch of an eyelid. Jacob, who had worked hard through the years to reach the point where he could legitimately describe himself as poker-faced, was prepared to acknowledge a peer. Then Gregorin smiled. But that didn't reveal much either.

'Lieutenant D'Agostino identified me as such last night. A KGB hit man, that is. *Et tu, Brute?*'

'Damn right,' Jacob said, having decided that some tactical push-and-shove was called for.

'I expected better of you than that.'

'Why? I mean, why should you expect anything of me at all?'

'Lieutenant D'Agostino is a bureaucrat. Bureaucrats come in an array of sizes, shapes, and nationalities—in Russia we are infested with them—but they all have one thing in common. They all have tunnel vision. You, my friend, are not like that. That's why Dimmie was drawn to you.' Slight pause for emphasis. 'And it's also why I know you know I didn't kill him.'

'What's that gambit's name?'

Gregorin crossed his arms over his chest as if to say he was prepared to wait indefinitely for a return to seriousness. It was the clone of a gesture Jacob himself employed under similar circumstances, and it irritated him to see it appropriated.

'It was Kaganovich who told me you're KGB. Are you telling me you're not?'

'What I am is a chess player and teacher. But I am also a Russian, and when my government calls on me for help from time to time I consider it a point of honour to oblige. Just as you would.'

'By government you mean KGB.'

'By government I mean a variety of ministries. I have also worked for the foreign office. And on behalf of what you might call the public relations effort. The list does not end there.'

'Did you once ask Kaganovich to go into the tank?'

'Into the . . .?'

'Deliberately lose a tournament.'

The smile of a man who has seen much history. 'Did Dimmie tell you so? Yes, of course he did. But surely you understood that side of his nature. He was a tremendous romantic. That was part of what made him so attractive. But it also made him totally unreliable as a reporter. Dimmie

hated the unvarnished truth. Truth, to him, was either
exciting or expendable. There *was* a tournament. We *did*
have a conversation. He *did* begin by playing poorly, salvag-
ing victory only through brilliance. After which he accused
me of . . . certain things. But as I say, that was Dimmie,
revelling in his own made-up drama. I never held it against
him. I liked him too much.'

'And Tsarkov?'

'Do you mean was he equally understanding and forgiv-
ing?'

Jacob nodded.

'Of course not. Tsarkov is a child. A giant when it comes
to chess. A child in virtually every other regard. A child
with a child's direct, uncomplicated response to any set of
stimuli. But then that of course is why I am here now, here
in the United States.'

'Why is that exactly?'

He shrugged. 'To watch over Boris. To see that he does
nothing—nothing at all—to embarrass his motherland.
This country of yours, my friend, is a place of pitfall and
temptation.'

'You're a baby-sitter, in other words.'

'*Le mot juste.*'

'And *have* you kept Tsarkov good?'

'I keep him under lock and key. That keeps him good.'
Gregorin smiled. 'He hates me for it.'

'Under lock and key last night around midnight?'

'From ten o'clock until half past seven this morning when
we broke our fast.'

'Can you prove it?'

'To myself, yes. I sleep with a cot against the door. To
Lieutenant D'Agostino, probably not. But to you, Jacob, I
say Tsarkov did not leave our room last night. I say it
emphatically, hoping you will believe me and help if and
when the situation becomes delicate.'

'Help how?'

'With the lieutenant. He makes noises as if it's in his

mind to detain us. That will draw the kind of attention to us we have so far managed to avoid, though this morning's newspapers contained a few bits and pieces of worrisome speculation. Who are Hatfield and McCoy, incidentally?'

'Not chess players,' Jacob said. 'Explain to me why I should get in an uproar about any difficulties you might have with Lieutenant D'Agostino?'

Gregorin sighed. 'I wish there was a better answer for that than the one I have.'

'Tell me the one you have.'

'You are sophisticated enough to appreciate my difficulties and large-spirited enough not to wish to add to them.'

Jacob waited.

'Also, since you are who you are, the lack of *quid pro quo* will deter you less than it would most men, myself included.'

Jacob, admiring the deftness with which he was being manipulated, found himself grinning.

Gregorin bowed in acknowledgement.

Jacob kept silent, thinking. Gregorin saw what he was thinking and said, 'Tsarkov did *not* kill Dimmie. He did send those ridiculous death threats, but I tell you as a man of honour he did not leave the room last night.'

'OK,' Jacob said.

'That means you will take my word for it?'

'Yeah.'

'And you will help with D'Agostino if it should become necessary?'

'I'll do what I can. It may not be a lot.'

Gregorin shook his head. '*You* may underestimate Jacob Horowitz, I do not. Thank you, my friend. You have saved my life.'

Jacob raised an eyebrow.

Gregorin smiled. 'Well, perhaps not literally. *Glasnost* is after all *glasnost*.'

'I just figured something out,' Jacob said.

'What?'

'How Kaganovich knew Tsarkov sent those death threats. You told him.'

'You are a clever man, Jacob.'

'Why did you?'

Gregorin shrugged. 'Because I wanted Dimmie to understand what nonsense they were. The instant he knew they came from Boris he stopped worrying about them. There is craziness in Boris. There is even violence in him, but never murder. Dimmie understood this as well as I do.'

Jacob believed there was murder in everyone, given the right set of circumstances, but he was not disposed to argue the case here. Sufficient that he was persuaded Gregorin's bed had been an effective barricade.

Gregorin held out his hand to be shaken. 'My government will be grateful,' he said.

'Is that right? Well, then tell it to close down Siberia and free all political prisoners.'

'Modestly grateful,' Gregorin said expressionlessly and took his leave.

Returning to the Postings board, Jacob learned: (1) that Tsarkov remained at the top of the Open section, five wins, no losses; (2) that Lanie had withdrawn from the tournament (no Dimmie, no reason for trophies in Dimmie's game?); (3) that Foxy Farrington was one of four left unbeaten in U 1400; and (4) that he, Jacob, had drawn a bye Monday afternoon and would be playing Farrington in the evening.

CHAPTER 6

It was about 2.30 when Jacob entered Barney's. The lunchtime crowd had thinned to half a dozen. These were quiet, serious drinkers, isolated from each other. In the dimness they looked like tombstones in an old graveyard. Barney himself, chewing on a sandwich absent-mindedly at the far corner of the bar, looked spectral until Jacob's eyes adjusted, and then he just looked sixty. Jacob went over to him, and without waiting to be asked Barney drew him a beer.

'You've got a fan in Rittenhouse Park,' Jacob told him.

'What am I doing with a fan in Rittenhouse Park? They got nothing but yuppies there.'

'What they got there currently is an open-air arts and crafts exhibition. And in this one not-bad painting a kid pitcher is blowing a high hard one past Dimag. Off in the background you can see the scoreboard, so you know it's an All-Star game.'

Barney smiled. 'Three pitches, never took his bat off his shoulder. A "K" to remember. I'd like to see that painting.'

'You will.' Jacob looked at his watch. 'At about four this afternoon it'll be delivered here. I bought it for you.'

Then Jacob told him about the young painter, the fan, whose father had pitched Triple A ball one golden summer before elbow surgery. Barney had been his idol, Barney's big high kick his pattern. The boy had grown up on Barney Hogan stories.

'When I told him I was buying it for you he didn't want any money but I insisted.'

Barney made a move towards his cash register, but Jacob grabbed his shirt front. 'Negative,' he said. 'Fifty bucks won't plunge me into abject poverty. That's all he'd take. He's framing it now, and I think you'll like it.'

'I think I'll be crazy about it,' Barney said, turning to examine the wall behind him. 'Slap it up there right next to Willie.'

Called away, he left Jacob surveying the panelling and trying, idly, to gauge the improvement the new painting would achieve. But all at once gears shifted, shifting Jacob himself from idle to overdrive. It was a response mechanism he recognized, having experienced it often before, and he thought of it now as *familiarly* mysterious. Some sudden pressure, some highly charged but usually unidentifiable stimulus triggered it. Adrenalin got to pumping. Sweat glands went into action. And as he stared at the portrait photo of Willie Mays he knew there was a connection he should be making. *With Willie, for God's sake?* Not *with* Willie. Not Willie exactly, but . . . Wheels spun unproductively.

Barney was back. 'Anything new on Kaganovich?'

Jacob drank some of his beer. 'Buddy says she was here past midnight.'

'I know.'

'You know what? That she was here, or that she says she was here?'

Barney swabbed the counter top. 'Both.'

'You saw her here?'

'Yeah.'

'You saw her . . . say from eleven until past midnight?'

Barney put the rag aside and met Jacob's eyes directly. It was the kind of icy gaze that had once given hitters something existential to think about. 'You heard me,' he said.

'I heard you, and you're lying to me just like she is. Why? Who am I all of a sudden—Judge Roy Bean? Adolf Hitler? What's going on?'

'You're fuzz,' Barney said.

'That's it? Just fuzz? I'm not the friend she's been telling me I am all these years? I'm just someone who has to be lied to?'

Barney shrugged.

Jacob slammed his beer mug down on the counter. 'Answer me, goddammit.'

Half the tombstones became animate and swivelled in response to the noise. The other half, impervious to any drama not their own, continued to stare into their glasses as they might have if Jacob had authoritatively announced Armageddon. To the heads lifted towards him Barney said, 'What's it to you?' And they turned to stone again.

To Jacob he said, 'There are different kinds of friends.'

'How different?'

'Some set limits, some don't.'

'What limits?'

'Tell me you wouldn't put the arm on her if you thought she'd burned him.'

'Thought?'

'Knew.'

'If I knew what?'

But Barney didn't answer. Half smiling now, he watched Jacob almost sympathetically. It was as if he'd found a slot in Jacob and could peer through it to follow the wrestling match he'd known would be in progress. It was an ancient contest; a contest of which Jacob had grown sick and tired, but a lot of good that did. It was also reflexive. Given a certain set of circumstances Jacob inevitably wrestled with his angel. Or to put the dilemma in less metaphoric terms— what did a man of the law do when friends or lovers went astray? A man of the *law*, mind you.

Not such a big deal, people were always telling him. Even Helen, a wavelength-sharer nine out of ten, saw this dilemma as medium size. To her, in the last analysis, the law was no more than an abstraction, a good thing in its way but demonstrably less urgent than flesh and blood. To Jacob, however, it was as if the law *was* alive. His devotion to it was not intellectual but passionate. Why be a cop, for God's sake, if you didn't love the law passionately? Just to break heads? In the past—Barney to the contrary—he *had* turned his back on it for the sake of a friend. Always he had done so feeling rotten. And always he had sworn never to do it again. And always . . .

Barney said, 'Jacob, Buddy gave you good advice—go home.'

Jacob stared at him. 'What are you telling me?'

'I'm not telling you anything except go home. Do it.' As if on cue D'Agostino now appeared in the doorway, and Barney lifted his chin towards him. 'While you still got a choice.'

'About what?' D'Agostino said.

Neither of them answered.

He took the stool next to Jacob's. 'Forget I asked.' Pointing to Jacob's glass, he said, 'One like his, please. Take 'em both out of this.' He put a five-dollar bill on the counter.

'His is on the house.'

'How come I never get one on the house? You don't like Philly cops?'

'Jacob's not a cop, he's a friend,' Barney said expressionlessly.

He drew the beer, then moved off down the counter, the publican on his rounds.

D'Agostino said, 'The gun *was* registered to Kaganovich.' And then without a pause: 'How come you never told me about the death threats, and I had to hear about 'em from the KGB?'

'Sorry.'

'You were going to tell me but it slipped your mind?'

'Something like that.'

'Anything else in that same category?'

'*Vaya con Dios, amigo,*' Jacob said. He mimed pulling something off his chest and slapping it on the counter. He started to get up.

Staring gloomily at the invisible deputy sheriff's badge, D'Agostino pulled him down again. 'Did you see the *Sentinel* editorial today? "A Call for Action." That was the headline. Where do they get off with that kind of crap? I mean, what action? Don't they think I'd bust someone if I knew who?'

Jacob kept silent.

After a moment D'Agostino said, 'You and your cousin Buddy go back a long time, right?'

Jacob nodded—warily.

'I mean a *long* time. Kids together.'

'So?'

D'Agostino pursed his lips thoughtfully. 'Kids go in for nicknames a lot. I had a cousin called me Dagwood Bumblehead. Dag for D'Agostino, you know?'

'Nice.'

'Buddy's a nickname, right?'

'Yeah.'

'Sure it is. Her name's Barbara. Aside from that?'

'No.'

'No pet names? You never called her princess or anything? I mean, that's a kind of common pet name for guys with kid cousins.'

Jacob looked at him. 'No, I never called her princess,' he said. 'And I never called her Queenie either. Or your royal goddam highness *King* Buddy in case that's your next question.'

'Just checking,' D'Agostino said, unmoved.

'What happened to the Soviet spy ring?'

'Somebody told me to focus on motives closer to home. Somebody a hell of a lot smarter than I am. So I'm doing that. Jacob, I ain't enjoying this, but it's called police work, OK? And the fact is her motive's classic A Number One. She had the hots for him, he married someone else. She wouldn't be the first woman who ever found that tough to take.'

'Tough to take is not pull the trigger.'

'Maybe that was an accident. They start to scuffle, accidents happen. I'm willing to see that as a real possibility.' He brightened. 'Hell, that'd be just fine with me. Who wants to railroad anybody?'

Jacob kept silent.

After a moment D'Agostino said, 'She *was* there, Jacob.'

'You've got a witness who'll say so?'

'I can place her in the hotel lobby.'

'I told you before. The hotel lobby is twenty-one floors below where you've *got* to place her. In addition, *your* witness could have been wrong. He could have just thought he'd seen her. She's got a witness who'll place her here.'

D'Agostino snorted. 'Barney.'

'What's wrong with Barney?'

'He's so nuts about her he'd lie himself purple if she asked him to.'

'So you say.'

'So everybody says.'

'What everybody says doesn't make a case.'

As if that were some kind of coda their fugue had been building towards, neither spoke for a moment. Twinned glances peered without interest into half-filled glasses, and then D'Agostino said tiredly, 'Yeah, but if I really could connect her to those friggin' kings, I swear to you I'd pull her in. And I'll tell you something else.'

'What?' Though he knew.

'Were you me, so would you.'

Infuriated by this universal eagerness to read his mind and predict his behaviour, Jacob put an ancient Talmudic curse on D'Agostino's head, got up again and would have stormed out, but Barney was approaching waving an envelope at him.

'Guy just gave me this for you. From Foxy.'

Jacob jammed it into his pocket.

Barney came with him to the door. 'Is he going to bust her?'

'Ask him.'

'I'm asking you.'

'I don't know. But if I did and the answer was yes, what would you tell her to do?'

'Something.'

'What? Fly to Chicago? Zanzibar? Timbuctoo?'

'No.'

Jacob felt his shoulders sag a little. 'God, maybe I would.'

But Barney's expression was curiously untroubled. Not a smile exactly, but at least the embryo of one. Watching it take shape, however, Jacob felt no inclination to match it.

'Cheer up,' Barney said. 'Nothing's going to happen to Buddy. You think I'd let it?'

Instead of answering, Jacob shot a glance at Willie Mays. Give, he ordered silently. But probably Willie didn't hear him, for he said nothing.

'About four?' Barney asked.

'Four what?'

'The picture, you damn fool. K-K fanning Dimag.'

'I forgot. Yeah. Four, four-thirty.'

Barney made the thumbs up sign as he moved back into the dimness. After a moment Jacob identified the unsettled feeling he was left with—the bottom step syndrome: where you thought it was, you suddenly knew it wasn't. With a final, furious, frustrated stare at withholding Willie, he stomped out of the bar.

Inside Foxy's envelope was a card similar to the one Jacob had taken from the bulletin board in Postings. This one, also, bore a message from *Kings II*:

> '... What peace, so long as the whoredoms of Jezebel are so many?'

CHAPTER 7

The *Sentinel*'s floor plan was ninth decade contemporary, which meant a chain gang of staffers' desks butted up one against the other, each humped by its own word processor. Copier machines, like guards fearing outbreak, were positioned at strategic intervals. On the rim of this gridiron-sized room was a touch of gentrification—a handful of offices for editors, columnists, and department heads.

Farrington, waiting at the door of his, bowed low. 'Such an honour,' he said.

Jacob passed Foxy without speaking.

His sanctum was large but spartan. (Precisely, Jacob decided, because it was expected to be flamboyant.) It contained desk and word processor in their customary symbiotic relationship, two wooden chairs, a small table, and a large bookcase. The bookcase was stocked impressively— not a frivolous title among the hundred or so on display.

All the books had been denuded of jackets, stripped, as of their decorations by a vengeful military court, and the cloth thus revealed was non-frivolous too, mainly dark blue, dull red, and foggy morning grey. On the table was an array of signed photographs—Farrington with a selection of the nation's great: Ronald Reagan, William Buckley, John Tower, Bob Hope, and Ollie North. In each of these Farrington looked unlike himself, and at first Jacob couldn't figure out why. Then he realized he had never before seen Foxy smile without rancour. Tacked to the cork board that served as a message centre, there were two three-by-fives:

> The chessboard is the world, the pieces are the phenomena of the universe, and the rules of the game are what we call the laws of nature.
>
> *Thomas Henry Huxley*

> The time is out of joint;—O cursed spite,
> That ever I was born to set it right.
>
> *W. Shakespeare*

Farrington motioned Jacob to a chair. 'But to what do I *owe* this honour?' he asked.

'I got the feeling you wanted to see me,' Jacob said.

'Did you indeed?'

'That's why I'm here. If I'm wrong, say so and I'll leave.'

'Touchy, touchy. Such a thin-skinned minion of the law, our Jacob. Well, I suppose we could discuss an interesting aspect of the Kaganovich case, one involving that woman next door.'

'What aspect?'

'A piece of information I've come by. Something she'd hate for me to tell Gene D'Agostino. Something that—'

Suddenly Jacob yawned. It was an uncalculated yawn, a yawn without a trace of ulterior motive, not intended to affront, or to bully, or to achieve some sort of psychological edge. The yawn had slipped out, simple testament to Jacob's having slept poorly since leaving the Tri-Towns.

But the effect it had on Foxy was galvanic. It enraged him. Eyes blazing, he was on his feet at once, finger pointing like a potential source of laser beams. 'Do I bore you, sir? Do I? Oh, what a mistake that would be.'

'Hey, there,' Jacob said pacifically. 'Take it easy, Foxy.'

'Don't call me that. That's permissible for my friends, but you're not one of them, in case I haven't already made that sufficiently clear.'

Jacob hauled himself up and started for the door. 'When you've got it all sorted out in your mind, you can send me another three by five.'

'You better wait,' Farrington shouted. 'You just better not go high and mighty with me, sir, or you'll regret it deeply. You think I'm crapping around about what I could tell D'Agostino? You're dead wrong. I know exactly what went on in Kaganovich's room, and Buddy Horowitz would kill to keep me from telling what it is.'

Jacob studied him. 'If you know so much I wonder why you haven't told already?'

That generated the kind of Foxy smile never seen by Ronald Reagan. 'What, and end her suffering?'

Then suddenly he jerked open the middle drawer of his desk, reached in and brought out a piece of letter-head stationery. Or rather the scorched top right-hand corner of one. Remnant though it was, Jacob had no trouble recognizing it. Nor the handwriting. It was Buddy's. He tried to read it, but what was left amounted to only a jumble of alphabet.

'Ah, but there's more where that came from,' Farrington said. 'Pretty sexy stuff.'

'Where did you get it?'

'Where do you think?'

'Were you in Kaganovich's room the night of his death?'

Farrington's grin grew wider. 'Jacob, you're just never going to know the answer to that. As far as you're concerned, that's just going to remain one of life's great mysteries.'

Jacob stared at him. Farrington met and returned the stare with all the bravado of a man who views his position as impregnable. Foxy had a firm grasp of the Horowitzian Code and the tenets of it that kept him safe. Barring heaven's intervention—and a miraculous augmentation of pounds and inches—Jacob would never lay a hand on him. Foxy knew he could stick and stab, tweak and jab with absolute impunity. Jacob was his, bearing his brand just as surely as if he had been born for no other purpose. Foxy allowed his lips to curl in a sneer and his whole expression to coil into that particular arrangement experience had taught him was Foxy Farrington at his most insufferable.

'This evening, Jacob,' he said. 'Like Grant took Richmond. Ten, twelve moves maybe. You'll want to die.'

Jacob started out of the room, but stopped. Then, teeth clenched, fists likewise, he stepped back and kicked the extra chair hard enough so that it ricocheted off the far wall and had to be eluded on its return trip. Concealing both the pain and the limp this caused, he completed his exit, accompanied now by the paradoxical sound of a fox crowing.

He looked into Buddy's office. She wasn't there. 'Damn woman doesn't earn her pay,' he growled silently and stomped out of the building.

It was about five minutes later that he began to suspect his cab had a tail. Green rented Chevvy. Driver and one passenger. Both male. Youngish, he thought, and clumsy at the work. He put the cabbie through two needless left turns. Chevvy performed similarly. Just to be sure, he had his driver double park next to the Penn Mutual building at Fifth and Chestnut. The cabbie protested, claimed he'd been ticketed in exactly that spot the previous week and that with him lightning made it a rule to strike twice.

'Police business,' Jacob informed him, flashing his magic badge. As usual, the frog became a prince. Jacob ducked

into the building, counted fifty, re-emerged, and there was
the Chevvy half way up the block, peeking from between a
raunchy Ford pick-up and a sleek blue Jag (kin to Dimmie's,
he thought with a twinge).

Rejoining his sulking cabbie, Jacob gave him Buddy's
address.

'Damn near ducked out on you,' the cabbie muttered,
getting under way: James T. Kelly—in his late thirties with
a dog-in-the-manger look to him that came with finding the
world a joyless place.

'No, you didn't,' Jacob said.

'Huh?'

'*Les Misérables*,' Jacob said.

'What the hell you talking about?'

Jacob didn't explain.

In the meantime the Chevvy had remained faithful to its
task.

At the apartment entrance Jacob gave Kelly a slip of
paper torn from his notebook with certain information on
it. He also gave him double fare. 'D'Agostino's a cop,' he
said. 'In thirty minutes I want you to call him and tell
him he can reach me at my cousin's. Tell him about the
Chevvy—'

Kelly was startled. 'What Chevvy?'

'The one on our tail. Licence plate noted.' He indicated
the paper.

Kelly's ears turned a belligerent red. 'What the hell's
going on here? I didn't see no friggin' Chevvy.'

'Kelly . . .?'

'Huh?'

Jacob thrust his head forward so that his nose and Kelly's
were all but contiguous. 'Here's what *Les Mis* means. It
means you're to do as you're told, exactly as you're goddam
told, or something my size is going to be tracking your ass
until you're ninety-five. Understand?'

Red was no longer Kelly's primary colour. Jacob thought
he would prove cooperative.

At the security desk he made further arrangements. He told the elderly guard that merchandise was about to be delivered to him (Jacob) in care of his cousin. He wasn't precisely sure of its description, but whatever it was he wanted no difficulty placed in the path of the deliverer.

The guard looked bewildered.

Jacob gave him ten bucks and watched his brow clear.

Half expecting to find Buddy in her apartment, he was delighted to be wrong. The apartment was empty. Police special in his lap, he sat down to wait.

Not long.

When the doorbell rang he answered at once. 'Yes?'

'Special delivery for—'

Smith & Wesson met occipital bone, and a chunky twenty-year-old with a beer-belly, a burr haircut, and an instant headache staggered back against the far wall and slid down it. His long-barrelled machine pistol fell from nerveless fingers.

'Jeeze,' his companion said. But that was all before speech was lost in a howl of pain. Jacob had stamped viciously on his instep. Instinctively, he bent towards it and was in turn bashed by the busy S & W. Older of the two but essentially the same build and tonsorial style, Jacob noted, as the battered pair braced each other like ill-used Raggedy Andys. In fact the resemblance was strong enough to be fraternal. Perhaps they *were* brothers, Jacob thought. Contracting, a family business.

He located the elder's weapon—a .38 calibre long-barrel, twin of the kid's. Nasty. He kicked both guns into the apartment and vacuumed their owners to see what else they were carrying. Pig-stickers and knuckle-dusters, evenly distributed. Leaning against the opposite wall, he waited for consciousness to return to one of them. He bet on the kid. He was right.

'Don't,' Jacob said as Junior indicated he might try to get to his feet.

'I was just—'

'You move when I tell you to. If I don't tell you to move, you're paralysed. OK?'

A trickle of blood was oozing down the side of his head. Junior wiped at it, hard guy style, as if it and hair tonic were indistinguishable. His eyes hated Jacob, made it clear this was to be a permanent state.

Jacob was undismayed. 'Speak,' he said. 'I want to hear your pretty voice. You plan to be good, right?'

'Yeah.'

'Sure you do. Because who likes bullets in the knees. Now help big brother into the apartment.'

'He aint—'

Jacob kicked him. 'He is if I say he is.'

The order was obeyed.

'On the floor, belly down,' Jacob said. 'You too.'

By this time Senior had achieved consciousness also but was playing possum.

'Who bought you?' Jacob asked Junior.

But it was Senior who answered. 'Nobody,' he said, a snarl. And then to Junior: 'You keep your friggin' mouth shut. We ain't—'

Jacob kicked him twice, sharply.

'Business type,' Senior said, a changed man. 'From out of town.'

Jacob only had to kick him once more (Junior twice) before they laid it out for him. Royal Rowell, of course, through certain West Coast connections. Five grand each. They weren't supposed to kill Jacob, merely maim him. Five hundred as a bonus for each major bone they broke, a hundred per finger.

D'Agostino's call came in just as they finished their saga. Jacob passed on what he'd learned and requested caretaking for the messengers. D'Agostino asked for their names.

'The Mudd brothers,' Jacob said and then elicited more accurate information: Joseph A. Renko and Nicholas L. Pappas. He forwarded this. 'A pair of beauties,' he said.

'Jacob . . .'

'What?'

'Any possibility they could have been a pair of Kings Saturday night?'

'Hold on. I'll put it to them. They love talking about themselves.'

He did—several times over—and was at length satisfied that this was not the case.

'Shit,' D'Agostino said. 'About Rowell . . . I could probably get him extradited, but it would be a pain in the ass. And my guess is he's got the lawyers to beat the rap.'

Jacob, the realist, acknowledged the truth of this.

D'Agostino said sympathetically. 'I'll send some blues for your friends, though.'

They arrived in a hurry, and as Junior was being released to their custody, he said, 'You'll be sorry you—'

But he never got to finish that either, this time because most of the S & W's barrel was in his mouth. Junior choked, eyes popping in terror.

'You're out of your league,' Jacob informed him. 'Tell him that, Bruv. Tell him how lucky he is to be alive.'

Thoroughly chastened, Big Brother nodded vehemently.

It was thirty minutes or so later, while stretched out on the sofa and in that limbo between waking and sleeping, that the idea came to him. He sat upright. Instantly he had recognized it as his liberating idea, the idea that would smash his chains. So shapely and craftsmanlike. Not merely functional but æsthetically satisfying in its utter simplicity. He took it with him to the kitchen. He poured coffee and sat down with it at the table, examining it for flaws. He found none. After a while he had no choice but to pronounce it brilliant.

CHAPTER 8

When Helen hung up, abruptly ending her conversation with Jacob, she had assumed it was George Adams at the door. It wasn't. It was Fielding Gow, looking even unhappier than he had earlier.

'What in hell does that man think he's doing?' he demanded.

'You caught up to him?'

'For a minute I did, but then he saw me and ducked around a corner. By the time I got there he wasn't. He's begging for trouble. I mean, I know this isn't South Chicago, but people get mugged in Oak Park, too. Honest to God they do.'

'Why don't you sit down and take a load off. You look all in.'

'Where's Deirdre?'

'Upstairs. Asleep, I think.'

He dropped into a chair. 'Hell of a night,' he said. 'What with one thing and another.' The grin that broke out changed his face from merely handsome (the kind of Greek hero profile you saw a lot of on old coins) to thoroughly likeable. As soon as he realized what he was doing, however, he stopped. Grins, he appeared to be saying, were not permissible to the Fielding Gows of this world, for what could be more ludicrous than a light-hearted loser? 'If something happens to him,' he said, 'I guess that'll be my fault, too, won't it?'

She didn't answer.

His glance fixed itself on the wooden floor as if something in its grain made it remarkable of its kind. His study was prolonged and apparently appreciative. Yet what he finally said was: 'Wanted to thank you.'

She shrugged.

Nervously, he pulled the loose skin at the base of his throat as if twanging a guitar. Helen winced though *he* seemed impervious—at least to that kind of pain. 'I don't thank people easily,' he said. 'It's been a long time since I've had to do it, and I guess I'm out of practice.'

She took the chair opposite him, leaning forward slightly to make eye contact. 'I hate whimperers,' she said.

'Whimperers?'

'You heard me.'

'Is that how I come off? I didn't realize I sounded that way. All I meant was . . .' He broke off. 'God, you don't give an inch.'

'This isn't about me. It's about you. And the abject way you feel sorry for yourself. And the implications of that. Would you like to know what they are? I mean as I see them.'

'Yes.'

'You're sure? Because next to whimperers and whiners what I hate most is talking just for the sake of hearing my own voice.'

He sat up a little straighter. 'Yes, I want to hear.'

'You're hell bent on wrecking two lives,' she said.

He waited for more, and when he saw it was not forthcoming he said, 'That's it? Short and sweet?'

'About a million miles from sweet.'

'Because she won't let me go? And if I go down she goes with me?'

'Not if, when.'

'No hope for me at all?' he asked after another interval of floor research.

'On what basis?'

'People change. You telling me I can't?'

She kept silent.

'I realize this is probably going to shock hell out of you,' he said, 'but I was a pretty good kid once. Yeah, I was— in high school. A's in math and science . . . All-League quarterback my senior year. I was OK. And then my old man . . .' He broke off, daunted by the complexities lying ahead in *that* direction. His old man . . . what? Died? Was killed? Killed himself? Made restitution? He shook his head, conscious at that moment of no one but himself. And when he finally spoke again he clearly considered himself on safer ground. 'My uncle, my guardian that is, was a flat-out son of a bitch.'

'Why are you telling me this?'

He looked at her, startled. After some further (though gentler) throat-twanging to underscore his own perplexity, he said, 'Jesus, I don't know. I opened my mouth, and that's what happened.'

'Why? Because you want me to start blubbering? What good's that going to do you? Or Deirdre?'

He got up, and without looking at her again climbed the stairs.

She poured herself some Scotch and sat sipping it until he returned five or so minutes later.

'She's beat. I made her promise to stay put if I went out again and searched for her father.'

Helen nodded.

'I told her you'd go with me.'

'OK.'

He shook his head. 'You really are a hard case, aren't you? Hard as they come.'

'Are we ready?'

But again that off-limits grin made it past the MP's. 'Even George Adams sits up and takes notice.'

'Does he?'

His nose seemed a bit puffier now than it had been, and he touched it tenderly. 'I thought he broke it. Probably would have, probably would have belted me again if it hadn't been for you.'

'Probably feels less sorry for you than you do.'

Somewhat to her surprise the grin withstood this, and when it went under a moment later it was not, she thought, a case of banishment in disgrace. 'Listen,' he said, 'I do

know what you mean about that. And honest to God, I am
beginning to understand what's at stake.'

'OK,' she said.

'And one of these days you're going to believe me.'

'I've got nothing to do with it. I keep telling you that.
And the longer we stand around here jawing about it, the
more I regret opening my mouth in the first place. You
know, or you don't. You'll change, or you won't. It's your
life. And Deirdre's. And neither of you mean as much to
me as George does. So why don't we get on out there now
and track him down.'

He opened the door for her.

It took them next to no time to find him, but when they
did he was not alone. He was about a block from his house
on a quiet, beautifully kept, tree-lined street, and—fulfilling
Fielding's prophecy—two young boys had him shoved up
against a high wire fence that circled someone's garden.

As they came around the corner they could see the moonlit
tableau—Adams clutching the fence as one of the boys
shook him down, while the other, the one with the hand
gun, directed the action. Both wore stocking masks and
gloves.

Fielding didn't even come to a full stop. He was instantly
into his wind-up, and from twenty yards out the first rock
was on its way. It hit the gun-toter in the small of his back.
His next pitch, a perfect strike, sent the gun clattering
to the ground. Sandwiched between the first and second,
Helen's ear-splitting Apache howl turned the decorous sub-
urban neighbourhood into a war zone. (Though nary a
window opened in response.)

Not proof against this combined counter-attack, the
young muggers fled, abandoning their arsenal.

Adams was dusting himself off as they came up to him.
'You ought to take that act on the road,' he said.

'You all in one piece?' Helen asked.

His clothes were a mess, and his hair needed combing,
but the rest of him seemed basically undamaged. Already

the mandarin features and steel-grey gaze had begun to assume their business as usual aspect.

'Scared hell out of me, but nothing to speak of outside of that. I got the feeling they were almost as scared as I was.'

'Virgins,' Fielding said as if he knew.

'They didn't exactly come as a surprise to you, did they?' Helen said.

He shrugged. 'Thought I spotted them back of the fire house about an hour ago, but I wasn't sure.'

'This kid's got more sense than you have,' she said, turning to Adams. 'He knows what's what in this day and age.' She toed the contraband Colt on the ground in front of her. 'Get one of these if you insist on nocturnal walks. Or start packing rocks.'

'Point taken,' Adams said, bending to pick up the gun.

'Good night,' Fielding said. He nodded, walked briskly away.

Adams glanced at Helen, who kept *her* face expressionless—a firefight had flared up in his. Brief but intense, and for a moment—Helen thought later—it truly could have gone either way. But then he broke into a jog.

'Hang on a minute,' she heard him call out.

At first there was no response. Fielding kept walking, and Helen could all but smell powder and shot from that combat area, too. At length, he slowed, stopped, and allowed the older man to catch up. After a moment they re-routed themselves and headed back to the house.

Feeling herself beginning to relax, Helen tagged after them. For perhaps the first time that night it occurred to her that the heavens, gleaming and glittering, were providing a truly bravura display. She thought about Jacob and wished he were there. He would have loved Fielding's brace of high hard ones, particularly the second, tailing off as it had to a classic slider before making contact. Not bad for a retired quarterback, she thought, smiling. Suddenly she stopped dead in her tracks, for just like that she had the distressing answer to Jacob's royal riddle.

CHAPTER 9

Jacob took his clock and board from the chess bag, then reached back in and got his pieces. He set them up, giving himself white, in keeping with the tournament director's instructions. Quarter of seven. Fifteen minutes early. Crossing his arms on his chest, he prepared to wait for his opponent, and in the next instant discovered he wouldn't have to. Resplendent in yellow straw, blue blazer, white trousers and matching shoes, Farrington swung into Cheswick like a man eager to collect a prize.

'Jacob,' he said, 'how very nice to see you.' Bowed and held out a three by five. Jacob accepted it.

> Chess, like life, is no game for fools.
> *George Santayana*

Incandescent foxy smile. Jacob decided then that the moment was ripe. Gathering a handful of Farrington's rich tropical worsted, he drew it towards him. 'There's this Apache I know, cousin's of my wife's. Little guy, littler than you, Foxy, who carries a great big hate for palefaces, carries it wherever he goes. Also he carries these shiny brass knucks, which he loves to use. Mean-spirited little bugger, Charley is. And as it happens he owes me favours.' Jacob paused for emphasis. 'Yeah, I guess you *could* call it kind of a contract. Open-ended, if you see what I mean.'

Loosening his hold, he allowed Farrington to straighten in his chair. Colour had left his face. Now, however, it was beginning to return. He was becoming conscious of the people around him. (Most of whom—being chess players—had managed to ignore the scene that had just taken place.) Moreover, Jacob could tell, he was beginning to think of things he might do to recover ground, working up to some table-turning, situation-saving. Foxy Farrington nastiness.

Jacob took a fresh grip on worsted. 'It's a new world, Foxy,' he said. 'Sensible behaviour is called for. Civil deportment and restrained manners. Charley's on notice. And from wherever he is, he can be in your office within twelve hours, he assures me. So walk on tippy-toes, Foxy.' He released him again.

'It's a bluff,' Farrington said. 'You're making it all up, and I don't believe a word of it.'

But watching him as he wet his lips, Jacob knew that wasn't true. Jacob smiled in satisfaction. A few seconds later they got the signal to play chess.

On his fifty-sixth move—by then the game was three hours and ten minutes old—Jacob, accepting the fact that a passed pawn had finally eluded him, resigned. Foxy chortled and was about to revert to type when he caught Jacob's look. His cheeks reddened, then paled. Finally green became his colour of choice, a remarkable shade of it—as if whatever it was he was swallowing had caused such severe intestinal ferment that mere biliousness would be a welcome step up. Reaching into his pocket, Jacob withdrew a three by five, which he pressed into Farrington's hand. It read:

> It's a new world, Foxy.
>
> *Charley Break-Your-Face*

Farrington's eyes were still rooted to the card when Jacob left.

Outdoors, Jacob took a deep breath. Canadian breezes had brought a respite, and the night air smelled sweet and good. He felt pretty good, too. He'd rather have won, of course, but he hadn't really expected to, and he was pleased with the way he'd hung in there. Things to work on, he told himself. Things to learn about the end game. A little more savvy with the rook and the king, and he might have had the fox's ears. It had been that close, closer than the little rodent had dreamed it would be. A year more of study and then he'd tear the Capa apart, he told himself, grinning. 'It's a new world, Foxy.' His grin widened.

Buddy was still not home when he arrived at her apartment. He was glad. It meant he could cling to his post-Foxy high for a little while longer. He poured himself a Scotch, kicked off his shoes and found some Mozart on the radio. But in a few minutes there was a knock at the door. He went to it, thinking Buddy must have forgotten her key. Thinking, as often before, that highs were defined by their fragility, or was it only *his* highs that broke at a touch. Thinking, gloomily, what in God's name was there to do about Buddy Horowitz's sea of troubles?

'You,' he said.

'Yes, yes, yes,' Helen said, fastening arms around his neck.

Hauling her up into his embrace, he staggered off with her to bed.

Later, in the kitchen by now, a decorous domestic twosome: Helen making coffee, Jacob watching. The reporter from *House Beautiful*, however, might have wondered a bit at his intensity.

'And it was a perfect strike, Jacob,' she said. 'And so suddenly I thought—'

He thumped his forehead.

She carried the pot to the table and filled their mugs.

He thumped once again. 'That's the connection I couldn't make. I kept staring at that photo of Willie Mays . . .' A third thump brought water to his eyes.

'Jacob . . . I am so sorry.'

'What the hell should you be sorry for? You didn't kill anybody.'

She covered his hand with hers, and for a while they sat there silently, each aware that the other was unwillingly tabulating, counting the ever-increasing number of ways they had witnessed in which essentially good people screwed up their lives.

Buddy found them like that. 'On little cat feet,' she said.

Swivelling, Jacob took in the running shoes, shorts, and sweaty T-shirt. Also the tension, underscored by the tell-tale glibness, always her camouflaging device.

'Wanted to see if I could sneak up on a pair of famous cops as easily as I did on Dimmie Kaganovich. And I did. Piece of cake.'

Helen found another mug in the cupboard, filled it, and brought it to her. 'Thanks,' Buddy said. And then smiled. 'Cool Hand Helen. Shirley always said you were a cool one. She hated you for it.'

'Shirley likes me better now,' Helen said.

'So do I, I think.'

'Sounds dumb, inviting you into your own kitchen, but come in anyway. Sit down with us.'

'No. Sorry. Not possible.' She looked at Jacob. 'There's an adversarial relationship to be maintained. One can't do that by going all *gemütlich*.'

'Adversarial,' Jacob said, and suddenly slammed his cup down on the table, hard enough to generate a minor cascade which had to be sopped up with his napkin.

'Jacob, darling, hypocrisy doesn't become you,' Buddy said. 'You *know* you're going to have to arrest me any minute now.' She cut off his protest. 'Tut, tut, no sophistries, please. You or your alter ego Lieutenant Gino. But I'm ready for you. I've done my jogging, which is to say I am now cleansed in body, mind and soul, and prepped for martyrdom.' She held out her wrists. 'Manacles, sir, whenever convenient.'

He got up, grabbed her shoulders, and jammed her not gently into a chair. 'We have some talking to do.'

'Jacob,' Helen said.

Angrily: 'What?'

'*Talking.*'

He stared at her for a moment. Then he sat down next to Buddy. 'I've been your friend since forever,' he said, voice noticeably controlled. 'I ask that you let me help.'

Pulling free, she at once started to cry, simultaneously

taking a roundhouse poke at his chin, which he just managed to move to safety. Helen shouldered past him, indicating as she did that for the time being the women might be better off alone. He withdrew to the living-room, while she slipped into the seat he had vacated.

Ten minutes later Buddy called to him. 'All right, shamus, you can return from exile now.'

She had washed and combed. Her eyes still showed traces of red, but she was clearly calmer. Actually, Jacob thought, she looked like a fighter whose corner person had done a good between-rounds job. The corner person was at the sink washing coffee mugs. She did not meet his glance. He gathered from this that he was on his own.

Buddy kissed his cheek. 'I'm sorry to be giving you such a hard time, Jacob, my darling, but the fact is I don't have a lot of choice, do I?'

'What's that supposed to mean?'

'Even a murderer has an obligation to survive.'

'You're a murderer? OK, who did you kill?'

She widened her eyes. 'Jacob, you haven't been listening.'

'Oh, for God's sake,' he said, turning to Helen. 'Now how am I supposed not to lose my patience with her? Back to Buddy. 'All right, have it your way. You killed Kaganovich? Tell me about it. Start with why you went to his room that night.'

'To get my letters, of course. You *know* he had letters of mine. Love-letters. Letters it makes my skin crawl to think of.'

'What were you going to do, beat him up, and take them from his senseless hands?'

'If I had to.'

'Or kill him if you had to?'

'Yes,' she said defiantly. 'It even crossed my mind that there was a gun in his room. He told me so. He kept it to protect himself from his father-in-law's goons.'

Again Jacob turned to Helen. 'You hear that? That's my

cousin Buddy, who once said to me the truth is worth dying for.'

Buddy started to speak but bit those words back and said instead, 'Not my fault if you won't believe the truth when you hear it.'

He glared at her. 'All right, enough bullshit for one night. Now I'll tell *you* what happened. You didn't go up there for the letters, Barney did.'

'He did like hell.'

'Shut up. It's my turn now, and you're to sit there quietly in your best-behaved listening mode. Either that, or Helen and I are out of here faster than you can say Jersey Turnpike, which is contrary to the *current* plan, isn't it?'

'I don't know what you're talking about.'

'How come Barney went? Because he overestimated how much you really wanted the letters back.'

'I did want them back.'

'Yeah, but not terrifically. Not the way Barney thought you did. If you did, all you had to do was ask, and Dimmie would have given them to you. Poor Barney. He didn't understand the complex little ex-lovers' game you and Dimmie were playing, not being an ex-lover himself. But then how could he be? He's still in love with the only woman he's ever been in love with—namely you. How long have you known that, Buddy? For sure, I mean.'

She didn't answer.

'What I don't have to ask is how long you've been feeling guilty about it? That's since Saturday night.'

For a moment he thought she might be going to cry again, but she didn't. Instead she took a deep breath and said, to Helen, 'What a drag it must be living with a man who thinks he's as smart as Jacob does.'

'Anyway there he was, laying it on the line. And when the answer he got was no dice, no letters, my guess is he tried to strong-arm Dimmie. Mistake. Nothing could have been more calculated to get Dimmie up on his hind legs and clawing back. Mistake? Hell, a whole goddam comedy of errors. I can see Dimmie going for his gun. And Barney trying to take it from him. And the gun going off, of course. And then Barney ducking for cover not so much to save his own hide but to keep Mother Teresa here free of the withering touch of scandal. And as for you, Mama T., you were in that hotel lobby, hoping to cut him off at the pass, hoping to keep him from getting into exactly the kind of mess he got himself into, but the timing went wrong, and he slipped by you somehow. Don't bother denying any of this because for one thing it's ancient history. It's now we've got to talk about.'

Buddy, who had been staring at the floor, head bowed as if in unconscious cooperation with some invisible executioner, glanced up sharply. 'Now?'

'You heard me.'

She looked at Helen. 'What does he mean? Does he mean he's going to help us?'

'Yes,' Helen said without much warmth. 'Couldn't you guess?'

The doorbell rang, and Jacob swore under his breath. 'D'Agostino. Into your room and keep that damn door shut until I tell you to open it. Understood?'

'Jacob . . .'

'Go.'

She hugged him. She started for the door and stopped. 'He regrets it bitterly, Jacob. You know him. You know that's true.'

'Big deal,' Jacob said and shoved her.

When he opened the door a moment later, however, it was not to D'Agostino but to Barney. His face was pale, but the blue gaze was as uncompromising as ever, fixed on Jacob's with the electric intensity that had always been his signature. A man who could make a fool of himself, yes, Jacob thought, but also a man who went his own way, obeyed his own code. And that being the case, not a man unduly concerned with consequences or regrets. If Buddy really believed differently she was dead wrong.

'Is she here?'

'In her room,' Jacob said. 'She'll stay put there. She thinks you're the law.'

He nodded.

'Do you have something for me to give D'Agostino?'

Barney drew an envelope from his pocket, and Jacob put it in his own.

Taking a cigarette from a crumpled pack, Barney lighted it like a man unused to smoking, which described him, Jacob knew. 'If I hung around it'd be the slammer for me, right?'

'Yeah,' Jacob said.

'I figure ten years.'

'Maybe. Maybe less. But yeah, it'd be the slammer. A man's dead.'

He blinked against spiralling smoke. 'Tell me about it,' he said. He produced a second envelope. 'This is for her. It makes her my heir.'

'OK,' Jacob said, taking it.

'Not that there's all that much to be heir to.'

'Twenty-four hours is what I was able to negotiate for you,' Jacob said. 'No more. After that he comes after you with everything he can put together.'

Barney shrugged. 'Who gives a shit. Just so she knows I love her. You'll tell her that, Jacob?'

'I already have.'

He smiled. 'And you, too.'

'You're wasting time,' Jacob said sourly. But then: 'Where will you go?'

'Zanzibar. Timbuctoo . . . Jacob . . .'

'What?'

'What the hell did those two kings mean?'

'None of your fucking business,' Jacob said in sudden, helpless rage.

'Yes, it is,' Barney said and waited.

'They weren't kings, they were K's, as in pawn to K-4, describing a move to a specific spot on the board. K's, for

K-K Barney Hogan, get it? Not goddam chess but friggin' baseball.'

'Je-sus,' Barney said softly.

'He made do with what he had, the hard-nosed little bastard.'

'Probably counted on you being around somewhere to figure it out. D'Agostino never could have.'

'I couldn't either. It was Helen.'

Barney grinned, shook his head, and left.

Jacob shut the door and leaned heavily against it. Helen came to him, put her head on his chest. For a while she listened silently to the jungle drum buried inside. Then she said, 'You knew all along it wasn't going to be D'Agostino at the door. How?'

'Because while I was out here exiled I called him and told him I'd see him tomorrow with enough answers to make him a hero.' He looked at her. 'She'd have gone with him,' he said.

'I think so.'

'Zanzibar, Timbuctoo, wherever the four winds blow. No guilt blacker than hers; no penance too great. And no life as valueless, right?'

'Yes.'

'I figured this was better. Was it?'

She kissed him.

THE END